MESSAGES, MEMORIES, AND MISFORTUNE

SOUTHERN SHENANIGANS

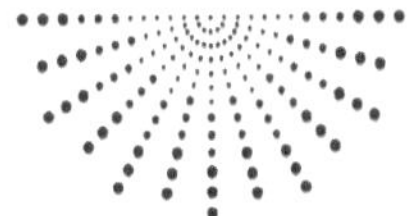

WINNIE REED

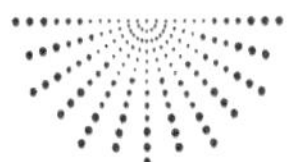

Frozen in place, Annie was shocked by the revelation her long-supposed father had delivered. Here he was, the man who had always been a myth hanging over her life, someone she'd thought about and worried about and even hated at different times throughout her four decades and then some.

This was the man who'd made it necessary for her mother to run, to take her daughter and get as far away as possible. He was poison, a pariah, a curse to anyone who knew him.

And here he was after all these years. To Annie, he seemed very small. And very afraid of the man she now understood was her real father: his brother, yet another family member she hadn't known existed until recently.

Strange how despite the roaring in her head, Annie heard Tyler get out of the rental car and slam the door. She was of half a mind to tell him to stay where he was, that it wasn't worth the trouble, but she couldn't find her voice.

Her real, true father had been in front of her, and she hadn't realized it. Too busy worrying about the mythical Cal Deacon to see what was in front of her.

Cal took a step back at Tyler's approach, eyes darting back and forth between him and Annie. "What is this? Some kind of shakedown?" He gripped his newspaper tighter, the envelope full of money he'd just received from his brother stuck inside.

"We don't want anything from you, so don't worry about that." Annie's apprehension rose as the two men regarded each other. She didn't want to step on Tyler's toes by announcing something she still wasn't sure he wanted to share. It wasn't her place, or so she told herself while the men eyed each other warily.

Suddenly, Cal snickered. "So you're him, huh?"

Tyler blinked rapidly. "Him?"

"Doris's kid. The one she said I fathered." He said it with all the casualness of someone commenting on last night's baseball game. "If this was thirty years ago, I could be looking in a mirror."

This was too much. Annie looked around in vain for somewhere to sit, but there were no benches nearby. *This is ridiculous. Get a hold of yourself.* She shook it off, using the irritation she felt toward herself and turning it on Cal. "You mean to tell me you knew about him all this time?"

Cal lifted a bony shoulder, his mouth twisted in a smirk. "She got a hold of me a few years after she had the baby, told me she gave him up for adoption. I don't know why she bothered. She didn't have any information about the people who adopted him, so it was a lot like closing the barn door after the horses already got out."

She glanced at Tyler, her heart aching at Cal's cavalier attitude. Certainly, she expected nothing less from him after everything she'd heard throughout her life, but this was Tyler's first direct experience with the man. And it wasn't exactly heartwarming.

Cal shifted his weight from one foot to the other, still looking around furtively as if he expected someone to jump out from behind a tree. "Can we take this elsewhere? I don't like being out in the open like this."

"Too bad." Tyler's fists, tightened, his rapid breathing, and it was clear he didn't care much for his long-missing birth father's peace of mind. "Both of us have waited a long time for answers from you."

Annie reached out and touched Tyler's arm, reminding him she was there. He wasn't going through this alone.

Cal looked across the street, where a coffee shop sat behind big, plate glass windows. "Let's go over there. It's a shame they don't serve anything stronger than coffee."

Yes, Annie could certainly understand the sentiment. She had never been much of a drinker aside from the occasional glass of wine, but even with the early hour in mind, she thought a glass of something very strong would be just what the doctor ordered.

Tyler practically had to be shoved into moving. He wore a shellshocked expression, and again Annie's heart went out to him. It didn't matter how old a person was, how much life they had under their belt. No matter how tough they believed themselves to be. At heart, all Tyler had wanted for years was to find his parents, to know where he came from. And here he was, all but rejected. A grown man might as well be a child in a situation like that.

It was still early enough in the morning that the

coffee shop was fairly quiet except for a few people hurrying in and out. There were empty tables near the back, and Cal led the way. At least he hadn't tried to shake them off.

The three of them sat without ordering anything, Tyler turning his chair around and sitting with his arms wrapped around the back like he was shielding himself.

Cal let out a deep sigh, slumping a little. "He would kill me if he knew we were doing this."

"Don't you think you're being a little dramatic? Why would he kill you?"

"You don't know the man. You don't know what he's capable of."

Annie leaned forward and folded her arms on top of the table. "You know something? My whole life, you've loomed large. I have to admit, I'm a little disappointed."

He looked her up and down and cracked a smile. "Take a number, sweetheart. I've been disappointing people my entire life."

"You sound proud of yourself."

He spread his arms, shrugging. "One day, I decided to lean into it, the way young people say nowadays."

She shook her head. "I can see why you have such

bad luck when it comes to gambling. You're a terrible liar. I'm sure people's wallets get heavier the second you enter a room." Tyler snickered but said nothing. "Why are you afraid of Gavin? Why would you not want to be seen with me?"

"You don't get it, do you? No, I guess you wouldn't." Cal looked her in the eye, and for the first time, his smile seemed genuine. "You look a lot like her. I always wondered."

The master manipulator at work, bringing up her mother at a moment like this. "Not enough to reach out or anything."

"That's the point. You just asked me why I can't be seen with you? That's why. My brother told me in no uncertain terms a long time ago that if I wanted to keep breathing, I would stay away from you. That's what I was trying to tell you about in the park."

"So, what? He's paying you off?"

"Generally speaking, yes. The money my brother so generously provides comes with plenty of strings attached. One of them is, I'm never to make contact with you. Or with anybody else in the family."

"Like your Aunt Hattie?"

Cal's brows lifted. "You know her?"

"No. She passed away before we could meet."

His eyes narrowed for a second, almost like he was wincing. "I'm sorry to hear that. She never much liked me, and that girlfriend of hers hated my guts, but I always did respect a person who lives their life on their terms."

Annie wasn't sure how much of this she could believe, so she ignored it. Meanwhile, all Tyler could do was stare at his father, and it was clear Cal felt the weight of that stare and didn't like it very much. He deliberately avoided looking at his son.

"I have to admit, now that I have you in front of me, I can't remember why it seemed so important in the first place. I guess I've always wanted to understand what happened, and my mother never told me. I've managed to piece enough together on my own, but I still don't understand this whole business"

"It's pretty simple. Your mother had an affair with my brother, then you came along. Happens all the time." Tyler made a choking sort of noise but said nothing. "And then she ran out on me. By that time I figured, good. I wasn't about to raise my brother's kid for him, and I didn't want to have anything to do with her anymore."

"Don't give me that. She didn't want to have

anything to do with you anymore because of the way you treated her. Both before and after she was involved with Gavin." Annie had the pleasure of watching him lower his gaze like he was embarrassed. "And we already know Gavin paid off some pretty hefty debts of yours. I guess that's how he's kept you under his thumb all this time."

"Look at you. A regular little Nancy Drew."

She saw his sarcasm for what it was and decided to be the bigger person rather than taking the bait. "Does he always deliver the money in person?"

"What, you think Mr. Important would take time out of his busy life more than once in a blue moon?" Cal snorted, bitter. "He was checking up on me. Wanted to tell me you were in town, and that if you found me, I was supposed to pretend you have the wrong person."

"Why?"

"You have to ask him that one yourself, I guess."

"Because he knows you're trash." Tyler was seething, his words barely intelligible thanks to how tightly he gritted his teeth. "He doesn't want you getting anywhere near her."

Cal's gaze slid over to Tyler, whom he sized up once again. "Nice meeting you, too."

"All right, all right." Annie squeezed Tyler's knee

under the table, glaring at Cal. "I don't think you can blame him, by the way."

After a few seconds, Cal snickered. "You're probably right. Anyhow, that's the long and the short of it. If I want to keep living a comfortable life on the right side of the law, I have to stay on the straight and narrow under my brother's terms. I'll spend the rest of my life under his thumb. Just the way he wants it."

"Or you could get a job."

Cal burst out laughing at Annie's reasonable suggestion. "Why would I do that at this point in my life? I've never had a proper job, and I never will." He said it like it was something to be proud of, but then Annie expected nothing less.

Everything was falling into place. Her father, her true father, had spent her life in the shadows, pulling the strings Cal had mentioned. That was a good way to describe it, too. The puppet master, hidden from view but controlling everything.

Now she knew who'd arranged for Norton's beating in prison. Who'd burned down the club she and Tyler had visited, only hours after they'd been there, probably in retaliation toward Joe for giving her the information she needed to find Cal.

And Melanie's college grant. It made her sick,

realizing Gavin had paid her daughter's tuition—certainly, it was the only explanation that made sense now.

It left her feeling dirty, even stupid for not seeing everything from the start. But then, how could she? All this time, she'd believed Cal was her father, and there had been no reason to imagine him doing anything so generous. What other conclusion could she have come to? It was easy to beat herself up after the fact.

She turned to Tyler. "Is there anything you want to say?" When he didn't answer, too busy glaring at Cal, she pushed back her chair. "I can leave you two alone if you want."

Tyler stood when she did. "I don't have anything to say." His voice was flat, empty.

Cal didn't make an effort to say anything to his son, and Annie supposed it was just as well. It wasn't as if there was anything the man could offer in terms of advice or support, anyway.

"Don't worry." She made it a point to look him in the eye when she said it. "We won't be bothering you again."

"Good. As it is, I'm sitting here wondering how I can explain to Gavin that I didn't do anything to put this together." He shot a look toward the front window, and Annie reflected again on how she had once believed him to be so much more than he was. No, it wasn't as if she ever had a high opinion of him, but she could never have imagined him so... Cowardly. Small, insignificant.

Tyler headed for the door with his hands jammed in his pockets, his head down. Annie trotted along behind him, then made a point of speeding past him on the way to the car so she could reach the driver's door first. No way was he in any condition to drive. He willingly handed over the keys before slamming himself into the passenger seat and immediately leaning over to turn on the radio. He cranked the volume up until it set her teeth on edge, but she withheld complaint. All things considered, this didn't seem like a terrible compromise to make. At least he hadn't done something foolish like taking a swing at Cal.

Though the man deserved it. It was like he didn't have a heart at all. No feelings, no tenderness, no empathy. No wonder he was so impossible to live with, impossible to love.

Even so, it was clear he was afraid of his brother, which only made Annie wonder what the man had threatened him with.

If Cal was afraid of him, as heartless and self-absorbed as he was, just how much worse was Gavin?

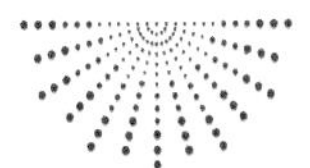

CHAPTER TWO

At least the trip home was less eventful than the trip to Texas. Annie's stomach had been in knots the entire time, praying they wouldn't have the sort of setbacks they'd experienced on the way out. She wasn't sure Tyler could keep it together this time, not after the disastrous meeting with Cal.

Since leaving the coffee shop, he had said no more than a few words at a time, and only when in response to a direct question. Annie was more than willing to give him all the time and space he needed, but all the while she knew there had to come a point when everything he bottled up would come rushing to the surface.

At least it hadn't come to the surface while they were in a plane thousands of feet in the air. Nor did it while they were waiting for their bags, and he actually seemed to be in a better mood as he loaded their bags into the trunk of the cab outside the airport. It was enough to give her hope that he might be able to get over his disappointment easily, painlessly.

Until they reached their block, where Sam's car sat in the driveway of the house they shared. Annie hadn't expected it, either—sure, he'd been looking in after Bogart, but like most cats, hers didn't require a lot of hands-on maintenance. Even if there was a reason for Sam to hang around the house, he could easily have walked from his house farther down the block.

Tyler growled softly. "I'm not in the mood to see that guy." There had never been much love lost between the two of them, with both men disapproving of the other.

"You don't have to. I'm sure he swung by to check in on the cat before heading down to his other place." He didn't live down the street from her full-time, only on the weekends, something Annie had yet to get to the bottom of. There was a lot about Sam she wanted to get to the bottom of. He was a nice guy, a great guy, but he had a habit of not talking much about himself. She hadn't forgotten about the young woman who'd come into the store, claiming there was more to Sam than met the eye. In fact, they'd had an argument involving that mysterious stranger the last time they were together.

Sam met them in the driveway, immediately taking Annie's bags. "I was checking on Bogart on the way out of town." He nodded to Tyler, who barely dipped his chin before continuing into the house without a word.

"Things didn't go well." She watched Tyler with a sinking heart. "I know he didn't expect much, but I'm pretty sure he still got less than what he was hoping for."

They went into the house, where Tyler had already gone to his room. Despite his mood, Annie couldn't help the tiny rush of pride and satisfaction at being back in her home. Hers, something she was building for herself. Whenever she started to forget how far she'd come since her divorce and the subsequent upending of her life, the house served as a reminder. She was a lot stronger and more capable than she'd ever given herself credit for.

To her surprise, Bogart sauntered out into the living room and even came to her when she called for him. After winding his way between her ankles, he sauntered off again. "Well, that's the warmest welcome he's ever given me."

"I can do better." Sam opened his arms and Annie stepped into the circle they created, allowing him to hold her for a second. It was good, even the simplest contact, and some of the tension she'd been carrying in her shoulders and back melted away. Still, there was too much left unsaid between them after their last fight for her to fully give herself over to the moment.

Stubborn? Maybe. But years of telling herself to let go of minor infractions committed by her ex-husband had left her jaded, less eager to dismiss her instincts.

Rather than go to her room and unpack right away, she sank onto the sofa with a grateful little groan. Sam joined her at the other end, and in a quiet voice she filled him in on their meeting with Cal. By the time she finished, he looked pained. "No wonder he's in such a bad mood." He cast a looked down the hall, toward Tyler's room, where the door was closed against the rest of the world.

He then turned back to her. "How are you doing? No offense to Tyler, but I'm a little more concerned with you."

The question took her by surprise, so much so

that she had to search for an answer. "Honestly, I haven't done much thinking about that. I'm all mixed up. I don't know what to think. All my life, I thought I knew who my father was—I might not have known him, but I knew him. Does that make sense?"

"Too much sense." He reached out and stroked the backs of her fingers. "But you realize that has nothing to do with you. The people we come from… We can choose them, but we don't need to tie our sense of worth to them, either. You turned out pretty darn well, all things considered. No matter who your father happened to be."

"Thank you."

"So, is that it? Are you satisfied?"

She told herself it was all in her head, the slight know-it-all tone in his voice. She was being reactive after too many days of stress, bouncing from one motel to the other, not knowing which end was up. Rather than pick up their fight where they left off, she offered the most honest answer she could come up with. "I suppose so."

He didn't quite believe her. She could see it in the quirking of his eyebrow, the upward tick of one corner of his mouth as if he was trying to hold back a smirk.

"It's not exactly as if I got any closure." Why she felt the need to defend herself was a mystery, but she did feel it.

He sighed and finally nodded. "I get it. And I can only imagine how frustrated you must feel. At least you're home safe. You were missed around here."

"Oh, really? Somehow I doubt the cat missed me very much at all."

"I wasn't talking about the cat." He winked. "My dogs missed you, too."

She rolled her eyes. "I have to pay them a visit soon."

"You'd better. You know how rowdy they can get when they have to wait for what they want."

"I doubt they'd get as excited to see me as they would their favorite treat."

"You'd be surprised." He stood them, stretching. "I better get going. I have a long week ahead of me. I guess you do, too."

It wasn't the right time to ask him exactly what he had coming up that week. He never offered very much about himself beyond the bare bones. "Yes, I guess I do. At least I know I can trust Rose and Lyle to handle things." Her great aunt certainly knew what she was doing when she hired them.

They hugged again on reaching the door, and this

time Sam brushed his lips against her cheek. "I would like to get together some night soon. Maybe we could go to dinner someplace."

"That would be nice." Because at the end of the day, the attraction between them hadn't gone away. In fact, now she regretted the tension and misunderstanding between them more than ever. What she really needed was to relax in the arms of somebody who cared about her, who would listen and understand. She wanted it so badly that she was almost willing to forget her misgivings for a little bit.

Then again, they were both adults and they both had things to do. She waved at him from the doorway before closing the door with a long, tired sigh. It was like she had aged five years in a few days.

At least the act of unpacking and getting her things together for the laundry was a distraction. Whatever she was thinking, whatever she was feeling couldn't get in the way once she returned to her regular, normal life. There were people who depended on her for their salary, not to mention the fact that the store helped pay her bills, too. Granted, she was not exactly a millionaire and probably never would be, but the place was a modest success that she hoped to grow and improve. She couldn't do any of that if she was too busy stuck in the past, asking questions for which there might not be any answers.

With the laundry basket balanced on her hip, she knocked at Tyler's bedroom door. "I'm going to throw a load of laundry in the machine. Do you want me to add any of your things?"

For a moment, she didn't think he would answer. Just when she was deciding to give up, he spoke. "No, thanks. And don't worry about fixing me anything to eat for dinner. I'm fine." He didn't sound fine, not even close, but she knew better than to push him.

It seemed like no matter how she tried to distract herself, though, there were questions that refused to go unanswered. Such as whether she should tell Melanie about any of this. Her daughter was a mature, level-headed person. Maybe a little too mature, with the sort of confidence only young people knew. Annie could remember well being that age, thinking she had all the answers, that she understood the world. Nothing could have been further from the truth. Here she was, with a daughter in college and a failed marriage under her belt, and there was still so much she didn't know.

The past weekend had proven that, for sure.

Did Melanie deserve to know the truth about her

college tuition? About the supposed grant that had made it possible for her to attend NYU in the first place?

Annie reasoned to herself as she finished loading the washer before going to the kitchen to rustle something up for a light dinner. The fact was, the idea of the grant being Gavin's doing was an assumption. Probably a very good assumption, probably pretty close to the truth, but she had no proof. The last thing she wanted was to ruin her daughter's trust by jumping to conclusions.

It would be better to contact the school and try to get to the bottom of it. Granted, that wouldn't change anything. She wasn't about to pull her daughter out of school over this. It felt only right to acknowledge the person who had made it possible for Melanie to attend her dream school.

Though even that wouldn't be enough to warrant a big, dramatic family reunion. Annie winced at the very thought while she fixed herself a sandwich. Never would she forget the fear in Cal's voice and body language when he talked about his brother, or what would happen if Gavin found out they were speaking. Annie wasn't sure her father was a man she wanted to meet, which meant she certainly doubted he would be a good influence on her daughter.

Then again, Melanie was becoming an adult. One day, she would have to decide for herself whether or not she wanted to meet her grandfather and thank him for what he'd done. Keeping it a secret would only brew resentment.

And if there was one thing Annie had learned through all of this, it was the uselessness of secrets. Eventually, the truth came out, and all a person could do was hope nothing blew up because of it.

What a cheerful note on which to start a new week.

CHAPTER THREE

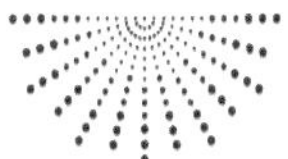

"So I told her, if she wants to see the book in stock, I can order it for her. Even that wasn't good enough. She told me we don't know what we're doing around here if we can't keep popular books in stock at all times." Rose shrugged, wearing a helpless sort of expression. "Meanwhile, I had never heard of the darn book."

Lyle scowled on his way back up from the basement, where he'd been picking through the second-hand books to replenish the racks out front. "People expect everything when they snap their fingers. Like the whole world operates the way Amazon does."

Rose scoffed. "I had a mind to tell her to go there if she was in such a hurry to find her book."

Annie had only half been paying attention up until this point. While she appreciated Rose and was happy to defer to her on a lot of things—such as understanding the personalities of her customers, most of whom Rose had known her entire life—rarely was she ever in the mood for gossip. And this story had certainly crossed the line into gossip, so she'd tuned out.

Lyle's comment snapped her back to reality. "Hush your mouth." She was only partly kidding. "We don't say things like that under this roof." After all, they already had their hands full, trying to compete against online retailers.

Rose brightened up on turning back toward Annie. "So how was your trip?"

Naturally, Annie hadn't shared the details of just why she was going away. "It was nice. We enjoyed ourselves." It was clear from the look on Rose's face that she wanted to hear more, but Annie was not about to give it to her. The entire town would know her private business by the end of the day.

Not that Annie held it against her. Rose was a well-meaning woman, but Annie had grown up in a place where it was considered impolite to either overshare or demand oversharing from others. She'd lived in North Carolina for months now and had yet to adjust to the well-meaning but somewhat pervasive need everybody seemed to have when it came to learning other people's private business.

Lyle snickered, seeing through his coworker's seemingly innocent question. "You might as well give it up, Miss Rose. She's not going to tell you what you want to know."

Annie turned her face away to hide her smile as Rose sputtered, insisting she had nothing of the sort in mind.

"I'm glad to be back. That much I'll tell you." It was something of a relief when a new customer came in, an older woman whom Rose instantly recognized and went to help.

Before Lyle could duck back downstairs again, Annie caught his attention. "Did anybody come in here looking for me? A young woman, maybe around your age or a little older. Dark hair, pretty. She came in one day last week, and I thought she might have come back."

Lyle appeared to think about this for a moment before shaking his head. "I don't recall anyone coming in and asking for you."

"Just checking." She was loath to ask Rose about

it since that would give her more reason than ever to show an unnatural interest in Annie's personal life. Besides, the fact was that Annie had no idea who the girl was or why she felt she had to warn anyone about Sam.

In a way, it reminded Annie of what she'd gone through when she first started suspecting Edwin of being unfaithful. Naturally, the situation was different this time. She and Sam hadn't done anything more than exchange a few kisses, after all. What stirred her memory was the way suspicion could take root and bloom into something twisted. She didn't want that for her and Sam. She didn't want it for herself ever again.

But it was there, that suspicion. Those questions. After what she'd been through, though, didn't she have every right to guard herself? Anybody in their right mind would be a little jumpy after a betrayal like the one she'd experienced.

Rose was still busy with her customer when the door opened again, and this time Annie smiled at a face that was familiar to her. "Detective Henderson. It's nice to see you."

Then she remembered Norton and the attack. Somebody had beaten him badly and had named her after doing it. While she would never consider

Norton a friend after he'd tried to kill her, never would she even have considered sending somebody after him.

Judging by Kevin Henderson's grim expression, she guessed his visit had to do with just that. "Glad to see you back safe and in one piece." He wore his standard shirt and tie, telling her he was on duty. This wasn't a social call.

She gave him her sunniest smile and hoped it look convincing. "Was there ever any doubt?"

"Do you want an honest answer to that question?" He held up a hand when she opened her mouth to protest. "Sorry. I didn't come in to start an argument."

"Exactly why did you come in, then?"

He lowered his voice, looking around like he wanted to be sure no one was listening. "I thought you should know he won't say a word about who did it. Not that we expected anything else. People in that position aren't usually eager to talk, unless there's been a threat on their life or something similar. He clams up and refuses to say a word."

Annie hadn't expected more than that, either. It didn't mean she wasn't curious. "How does something like that happen?"

"What do you mean?"

"Well, how would somebody on the inside be chosen for a job like that? If somebody's in jail, how does the person who wants the beating carried out arrange for it?"

"Getting any ideas?" He chuckled when she scowled at him. "We really don't know in this case. There are lots of ways for folks on the outside to ask favors of those behind bars. The message could be passed through a visitor. Heck, there've been cases where people have deliberately gotten themselves arrested just to get to somebody inside."

"Sounds like an awfully big risk to take."

"I agree, which is why the sort of people we're talking about are handsomely rewarded."

"You mean you think somebody paid him to do it?"

Kevin tipped his head to the side, frowning. "You seem very concerned about this."

"Why shouldn't I be? Somebody's out there beating people in my name. The way you made it sound over the phone just a couple of days ago, there were people in your department who thought I was the one who set the wheels in motion."

"Nobody thought that."

Annie had her doubts, especially when he averted his gaze. "I can't help but feel guilty, is all."

"Only you would feel guilty because the man who tried to kill you ended up getting the beating he deserved." It was the first time Kevin had admitted he thought Norton deserved what he got, a fact that was not lost on her. It probably wasn't the most professional thing he could've said, but she appreciated the fact that he cared just the same.

"The kid didn't stand a chance. He was raised by people who twisted him up." After Norton's father had committed suicide—in front of his son, no less—Norton's grandparents had blamed the tobacco executives behind his losing his job. Norton had been raised to believe they were the cause of all his troubles, which had inevitably created a thirst for vengeance.

"I don't disagree with you. But I don't normally hear that kind of talk from victims."

"There's your first mistake, Detective." She stood up a little straighter, looking him in the eye. "I'm not a victim."

"No. You certainly are not." He held her gaze for a beat before clearing his throat. "Anyway, thought you'd want to know."

Annie smiled even as her insides churned. What was she thinking? She should tell him about Gavin, shouldn't she? Would it be considered withholding information if she didn't?

Then again, she had no proof. Only a theory. A good theory, probably right on the nose, but still. The police couldn't pay credence to every little theory.

Besides, what could Kevin or any detective do? A man like Gavin would certainly know how to cover his tracks. In all, it was better to stay quiet.

Kevin touched his fingers to his forehead in a makeshift salute. "It's good to see you back. Hope you had a good trip."

"Don't bother, Detective." Rose looked downright doleful. "She won't tell you anything about it. I tell you, it's like pulling teeth with this one."

Annie very much had the idea that the detective and she agreed when it came to the overabundance of gossip in their little town. Still, for Rose's sake, he laughed.

"Some nuts are too tough to crack." He gave Annie a wink before leaving, chuckling to himself.

At least Annie didn't feel quite so much like a fish out of water when there were other, reasonable people around to tell her she wasn't alone.

She couldn't help but wonder as she watched

Kevin walk to his car just how much he would be willing to tell her about Sam. They weren't friends, that much was for sure—at best, she had picked up a hint of resentment between them the few times they'd been in the same place at the same time. Their civility was cool, clipped. Not for the first time did she wonder why. Did Kevin know something about Sam that she didn't? Maybe it was just the fact that Sam was a private investigator, and police officers didn't appreciate civilians sticking their noses into investigations. The more she thought about it, the more sense it made. Not everything had a deep, dark explanation.

Rose finished ringing up her customer before gasping. "I forgot to tell you. That girl came back in, the one who was looking for you last week."

Annie's pulse picked up speed. "Did she say why she wanted to see me?"

"No. Honestly, I think it was pretty rude of her. She practically threw a fit when I told her you were out of town, then started asking all kinds of questions about when you'd be back."

"I wish I knew why."

Rose chuckled. "You know how young people are. They get an idea in their head and nothing else matters. I'm sure whatever it is, it seems very important to her."

This hardly gave Annie relief. For someone who seemed to live on gossip, Rose didn't seem very interested in this stranger. "Do me a favor. If she ever comes in again when I'm not here, give me a call."

"Would you want me to put you on the phone with her?"

"No. I'm more interested in keeping track of how many times she comes in. I mean, I've already spoken to her, and she didn't give me much of an explanation as to what she found so important."

"Maybe she can't say. Maybe she was friends with you-know-who." Rose said this in a whisper, eyeing the door leading down to the basement, where Lyle had once again disappeared. He and Norton had been on friendly terms, and Annie understood her employee had nothing to do with the break-ins or the attempt on her life. Still, the young man had been stunned to find out someone he'd known for years was capable of murder. It was better for everyone involved if they didn't mention Norton in front of Lyle.

Annie hadn't told Rose what the strange girl had said to her when she visited the store. She didn't know this had anything to do with Sam, thank goodness. She made a mental note to be careful since gossip of this magnitude could blow up in the blink of an eye.

The quieter she could keep this, the better for all of them.

CHAPTER FOUR

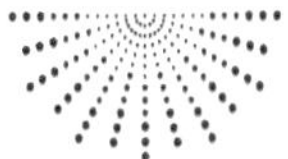

"That piece of slime." Mildred Asquith set her teacup on its saucer with perhaps a little more force than was necessary. Annie winced as the delicate china clinked hard enough to make her wonder if it hadn't been chipped. "You know as well as anyone what a low opinion I have of Cal, but I had no idea what he was capable of. How could he be so cruel?"

"And to his own flesh and blood, no less. I can't imagine."

"So he didn't try to deny the possibility of being Tyler's father?"

"Are you kidding? He made it sound like he'd been waiting to be tracked down all this time. He didn't care. He never tried to find his child, and when his child ended up right in front of him, he shrugged it off." It was enough to make Annie's blood boil, remembering how Cal had dismissed Tyler so coldly.

"The man is a piece of filth. I always knew it." Yes, and Cal knew she knew it, too. Annie had to bite back a smile, knowing Mildred had gotten her opinion across. "He's a narcissist, plain and simple. Hattie always used to say so. It's not possible for him to care for anyone but himself."

"I wish we had never gone." Annie sipped her sweet, fragrant tea. It didn't do much to soothe her spirits.

"That's easy to say now, but you had to go. You had to learn these difficult things. Now you can move on, move past them. You don't have to wonder anymore."

"Don't I?" For Mildred's sake, she held back a laugh. "Now, I have a father out there who's made it his mission to… I don't know. Protect me? Even though I've never asked a thing of him and didn't know he existed until now."

"Let me ask you a question." Mildred's mouth tightened into a thin, grim line. "If the man has been part of your life without you knowing it all this time, does knowing about him now have to change anything? You have a choice here. You don't have to think about him."

Annie blinked slowly, processing this while staring at her friend. "You mean I should pretend I never learned about him? I should feign ignorance?"

"Why not? You didn't know about him before this, and your life has moved smoothly—on the whole. There've been bumps, but every life includes bumps. What changes now that you know he exists?"

"For one thing, the more I think about it, the more manipulated I feel. Like a fool."

"That's up to you. From where I'm sitting, it sounds like you need to let yourself off the hook. Nobody thinks you're a fool."

"No." Annie rubbed her tired eyes. It had been a long day at the store. Naturally, she'd welcomed the patronage, but now the hectic hours were taking a toll. "Only me."

"Which is why I say you have to give yourself a little grace. And then you need to decide if this is worth it." Mildred's fingers twisted together in her lap, signaling her anxiety.

"You want me to stay away from him."

"Frankly, I do." Mildred looked and sounded apologetic, but firm. "He's not a good man. No matter the way he makes himself appear to the rest of the world. All those charities he funds and the like." She scoffed.

"He's never tried to hurt me, though."

"That's true. He has harmed people who've hurt you, though, hasn't he? Who's to say he wouldn't decide to give you the same treatment if you deny him somehow? If he wants the two of you to be close, to build a relationship."

Annie was about to remind her friend that Gavin had always kept himself in the shadows, that he'd never tried reaching out to her before. That there was no chance of him wanting anything more now. Something wouldn't let her do it.

There was never any telling with a man like him. He might decide on meeting face-to-face that he wanted to be a father to her or a grandfather to Melanie. Was that a risk she was willing to take? Could she gamble with Melanie's well-being like that?

"I see what you mean. For the record, I don't intend on searching for him. I'm worried about what my daughter will think when she learns she had a grandfather out there all this time, guiding her life the way he did mine." She bit her lip, her heart clenching at the thought.

"Does she have to know?" When Annie gave a

surprised start, Mildred clicked her tongue. "There's lying, and there's remembering that children don't necessarily need to know everything there is to know."

Annie chuckled. "I'd like you to say that to Mel, and I'd like to be in the room when you do it."

"Sure enough, I doubt she'd like hearing it—but that doesn't mean it isn't true. Parents have all sorts of reasons why they hold certain things back from their children. And it's generally for their sake." Mildred lowered her brow, lips pursed. "Did your mother feel the need to be completely open with you?"

Annie bristled. "No comment." If she had, this might've been avoided.

"She had her reasons. Much like you'd have yours if you chose to keep this from your daughter."

"I see what you mean." Annie gazed out the window, into the darkness. Her reflection was plainly visible, and in it, she noticed her worried expression. She'd start developing brackets around her mouth if she didn't stop frowning so much. "Things are already sticky between us. I know she loves me, but she carries resentment from the divorce."

"Children these days. So opinionated."

Annie snickered, turning back to the friend who'd become something of a surrogate mother since her arrival in town. "Tell me about it."

"In the end, you can only do what feels best to you. She'll understand in time, no matter your decision." Mildred scoffed at herself, grinning. "Listen to me. You'd think I raised children of my own."

"You were a child yourself once. I think that makes you qualified to weigh in on this." Annie gave her a grateful smile. "Thank you."

"You know it's a pleasure, having you here, talking with you. You're my connection to the outside world—you and Tyler, that is."

There went the frown again. "I wish I could help him. There's a brick wall around him now. I can't get through."

"You have a loving heart, but it's the loving hearts that are most easily wounded. Don't make the mistake of taking his pain on your shoulders. There's enough on your shoulders already." Mildred brightened. "I did manage to spread the word of his new business, though. A couple from down the block caught me as I poked my head out to get the mail, asking who'd done the work on the porch. I made sure to brag about him."

"That's great. I'm sure if he has something to turn

his mind toward, he'll feel better." That was what Annie hoped, anyway. She finished her tea and said her goodbyes, promising to have Tyler reach out to Mildred soon.

Even if she hadn't arrived at any conclusions when it came to handling Melanie and the tuition situation, Annie's spirits were considerably higher and lighter when she got in the car and started for home. Mildred had a calming way about her—the ritual of tea and cake or cookies didn't hurt, either. A few quiet, precious minutes in the middle of what sometimes felt like chaos.

Traffic was light as always at this time on a weeknight. There wasn't very much to do in their corner of the world past seven or eight o'clock aside from eating at one of the chain restaurants scattered around. By nine-thirty, when she left Mildred's, there was hardly another car on the road.

Except for the one behind her.

Annie hadn't noticed it and likely wouldn't have if it hadn't been for a bump in the road that made the trailing car's headlights bounce and catch her eye in the mirror. She dismissed it a moment later but noticed the car following her when she turned.

"You're making up reasons to be paranoid now." The laugh she gave herself sounded hollow and forced. In her gut, she knew something was off. Another random turn and once again, the car turned to follow.

Her palms went slick with nervous sweat and now she regretted the second cup of tea as it sloshed around in her nervous stomach. There she'd been, imagining her troubles being over once she'd left Texas. Was Gavin following her now? Or, rather, having somebody else do it for him?

She couldn't lead whoever it was back to her house, that much was for sure. Rather than follow the familiar route, she headed deeper into town, where there'd be more people around. The lights from a strip mall parking lot glowed promisingly in the distance and she followed them with her heart pounding.

Gavin had never tried to hurt her. That was something she repeated to herself as she drove, one eye always on the pair of headlights behind her. It was impossible to see who was behind the wheel, making it easy for the worst imaginings to take root.

By the time she reached the parking lot—still with that mystery car behind her—Annie's fear had begun to look more like resentment. She was entitled to live her life. She wasn't bothering anybody, wasn't asking anything from anyone, or threatening anybody's way of doing things. If her father wanted to control the world from the top of his ivory tower, he could do that as far as she was concerned. So long as he left her out of it.

That resentment was what made her pull into an empty spot beneath a light and step out of the car, purse over her shoulder. She still carried her pistol inside and was glad of it as her pursuer came to a stop a handful of yards away. Now that she was no longer blinded by headlights in her mirror Annie recognized it as a very sleek, very expensive BMW. Not the sort of car she'd expect a thug or leg breaker to drive.

She slid a hand into her bag, her fingers closing around the pistol, as the door to the BMW opened. There was no hope of taking a deep breath with her chest so tight, but she did her best to appear brave as the driver stepped out.

"You?" Her eyes widened at the sight of the girl who'd approached her about Sam. The last person she'd expected to see. "What are you doing? Why were you following me?"

The girl flipped her hair over one shoulder, an insolent gesture Annie recognized after witnessing it from her daughter a few times too many. "You're not an easy person to get a hold of."

Annie's exasperation was about ready to burst into flame. "That's not an answer. Why did you follow me? Were you waiting outside my friend's house all that time?"

"I wanted to talk to you without a bunch of people around. Like at your store." The girl folded her arms and glared as if she was the one who'd been scared half to death.

"You have my attention—but let me warn you straight out that if it's Sam you've gone to all this trouble over, you might as well save yourself the time. I have no desire to talk about him with you or anybody else. His personal life is his business." Where had that come from? Granted, it was the right thing to say, but it didn't exactly express Annie's true feelings on the matter.

The girl gaped at her. "You seriously don't care that he's a liar? And a thief?"

"A thief?" Annie couldn't help but bark out a disbelieving laugh. "Get out of here."

"Fine. If that's how you feel about it, maybe you don't deserve to know. Some people don't want to be helped." Now the stranger wore a twisted expression, bitter and cold. "Good luck with him. I hope he doesn't steal from you the way he did from me."

With that, she slid behind the wheel again and gunned the engine before peeling off, tires squealing.

Only then did Annie remember she hadn't gotten the girl's name or any indication of what her relationship with Sam had entailed. He'd said something about her being an ex of his, hadn't he? When they'd argued at his house. The argument was a blur now, the specifics unclear.

If she was his ex, he liked them young. This didn't exactly grant Annie a lot of comfort as she returned to the car and headed home, wishing she'd at least gotten a vague idea of who the girl was and why she found it so important to tank Sam's personal life.

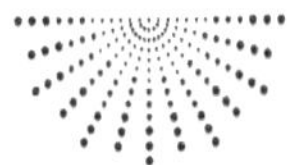

CHAPTER FIVE

It was early afternoon when Annie pulled up in the driveway with groceries in the back seat. She'd gone out of her way to buy things she knew Tyler liked, all in an effort to shake him out of his funk. No matter how correct Mildred was when she'd warned Annie against caring too much, the woman didn't live with him. Sharing a house with a virtual ghost wasn't exactly a pleasant experience.

He joined her in the kitchen, helping her put things away without saying a word. He wasn't slamming things around, which she took as a positive sign.

"Did you give Mildred a call this morning?" She took pains to keep her tone light and conversational.

He nodded, his back to her. "Yeah, she gave me

the number for those neighbors of hers. Said they were complaining about a leaky roof."

"Okay, that's good. Another job for you, if you want to take it."

"I get it." He closed the fridge before whirling on her with a sullen expression. He was wearing the t-shirt she remembered seeing on him yesterday and was in need of a shave. It was the beaten look in his eyes that struck her hardest, though. "You're trying to remind me there's more to life than having a parent who gives a damn I exist. I appreciate you caring, but you don't have to mother me."

She flinched under his sharp words. "I didn't know I was mothering you. I'm sorry if I came on too strong. But I didn't ask Mildred to recommend you, either."

"I know, but you know what I mean. You don't have to prod me along. I can take care of myself."

"I'm sure you can." Annie offered a tiny smile. "Would it be mothering if I asked whether you want something for lunch? I was going to make a salad for myself and could easily double it."

He wrinkled his nose. "No offense, but I was never much of a salad eater."

"I bought plenty of things I know you like, just in case." She pulled salad ingredients out at random, hungry after all that time at the store. "They always say to never go to the supermarket on an empty stomach, don't they? I proved the saying correct today. We have enough to feed an army, I think."

"Thanks for always being on top of things. I should be a bigger help around here."

"You're already a big help." When he snickered, she insisted. "Living with a man in the house gives me peace of mind. I didn't know how much I'd come to rely on Edwin until the divorce. Being alone, especially in a new place?" Especially with every-thing that had gone down shortly after she'd moved in. It made her shiver.

"That's not enough, though. I need to be bringing in more money to help with the bills and food and everything."

"And you will." She flashed a confident smile. "I know you will. You'll get on your feet."

"Sure I will." He put a frozen mac and cheese in the microwave. "It's in my genes, isn't it?"

Annie closed her eyes for a second and counted to five in her head with her back to him. Anything she said now would have to be done thoughtfully, not off-the-cuff. Her voice was softer, cautious when she spoke. "You aren't him."

"But you've got to admit, our lives aren't that different. We've both been in trouble."

She waited, still turned away from him, not bothering with the salad now. "And? What other similarities are there?"

"We both know how to navigate shady places and shady people."

"Okay." Silence stretched out between them. "Anything else?"

"Don't do that."

She turned around and pointed at him. "You started it. You're the one who wants to compare yourself to Cal. I didn't go there. I never would."

"Come on." He rolled his eyes, eyes which now that she'd met Cal in person were obviously passed down from his father. Eyes that could go cold and hard in no time.

There was a difference, though. A very big one. "You would never do the things he's done. You don't step on people without a thought for them. You aren't self-absorbed the way he is. You have a heart."

"True." He said it grudgingly like he didn't want to agree.

"You want to do the right thing. And you don't use people the way he does." Annie shrugged before turning back to her lunch preparation. "I could keep going, but I'm starving half to death. And let's not even start talking about fathers. Mine is a piece of work, too."

"Also true." He opened the microwave and removed his plastic dish, careful not to burn himself with the steam as he lifted the film over top. "Looks like we both got the short straw when it comes to dads."

"You had a good father, though. Your adopted father. It sounds like he was a good man." She clamped her mouth shut tight before what was on her mind tumbled out. *Why can't you forget Cal and remember him, instead?*

"The best." Tyler sighed. "You're saying it's wrong of me to think so much about Cal, aren't you?"

"It's not wrong. I would never say that. Of course, you're only human. You're entitled to want to know who you came from." She poured a little dressing on her salad—then thought again and added more. If she had to eat rabbit food, the least she could do was make it palatable.

The two of them weren't exactly on touchy-feely terms, but right then it didn't matter. Annie took his face in her hands and gave him a stern look she normally reserved for her daughter. It was different, looking up at the person she admonished. "You have a family now. Me. Melanie. Even Mildred. I'm fairly sure she's determined to adopt you as her grandson whether you want her to or not."

He chuckled. "She's a good lady."

"She is, and she wouldn't waste time on anyone unworthy of it. We're here for you. You aren't alone in the world. Get out there, build yourself a business, build a life. I know you can do it." She patted his cheeks before turning back to her lunch, which she wanted a lot less now that she could smell the macaroni and cheese.

It still didn't feel like enough, though. Annie chided herself as she started in on her salad. If she spent all of her time worrying about the people around her, she would have nothing to give herself when she was the one in need. It was an age-old story, and she doubted she was the only woman who knew it by heart. Sometimes, it was easier to focus on other people's problems than it was to take a clearheaded look at her own.

That didn't stop her from setting down her fork with a tiny gasp. "Why don't you come up to New Jersey with me?"

"More travel?" Tyler lifted an eyebrow, setting his mouth in a wry smirk. "You aren't tired of traveling with me by now?"

"It would only be for a weekend."

"Which is exactly what our last trip was supposed to be. Just a simple, weekend excursion."

"This would be a lot more relaxed. I've been trying to come up with a weekend to drive up and visit Melanie before Thanksgiving since she'll be with her father over the holiday." The bitter taste in her mouth was not from the arugula she'd loaded onto her plate.

"That's not for me." He stabbed a few noodles probably harder than he needed to. "You should be spending time with your daughter, just the two of you."

"That doesn't mean you can't come out to dinner with us. I know she wants to meet you."

"She wants to take a look at me, you mean."

He was bound and determined to be negative. A smarter person might have taken this as an invitation to be left alone, but Annie had never been particularly smart when it came to the things she wanted. Once she got an idea stuck in her head, that was the end of it. Everybody else might as well get out of the way.

"So what if she wants to take a look at you? Who could blame her for that? Her mother is sharing her house with a stranger—a relation, but still a stranger.

I know it would make her feel better to meet you in person and see what a nice guy you are."

His mouth twitched. "You have a very generous way of looking at me."

Generous and stubborn. Yet another thing she set her mind on: the fact that he was a good person, and anyone who didn't think so simply didn't know him. "Stop being so down on yourself. I'm extending a hand to you, welcoming you into my family. I know you don't see it this way, but when you keep putting up walls, it's easy to take personally."

"That's not what I was going for." His face fell a little. "I don't want you to think I don't appreciate everything you've done for me. If anything, it makes me feel a little pathetic."

Looking at it from his perspective, Annie could understand what he meant. "I'm sorry. Sometimes when I want something, I can come on a little strong. If I'm pushing too hard, just tell me so. I mean it. It won't hurt my feelings." That wasn't precisely true, but she forced a smile, anyway.

"Can I think about it?"

"Of course. Besides, you want to schedule any upcoming work around a visit to New Jersey." She picked up her plate and headed for her office. "Keep in mind, this would be a favor to me."

"How so?"

No matter how cheerful she tried to sound, she could hear the strain in her voice. "It would be nice to have someone to help me as I go down memory lane." The notion of driving through New York made Annie's blood pressure rise. It would be better to have Melanie meet them partway, but it would mean brushing up against old memories in her home state, too. Still, it didn't seem like a bad idea to treat her daughter to a meal at what used to be their favorite restaurant back before things went sour.

Annie corrected herself. Back before she'd known things were sour. Edwin had pulled the wool over her eyes for a long time, leading both his wife and his daughter to believe they lived in a family quite unlike the one he secretly created with his lies and his cheating.

Having another adult present was just what Annie needed.

No matter what her daughter thought about it.

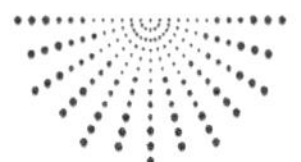

CHAPTER SIX

With Sam back in town for the weekend, it seemed only natural to swing by his house on Friday night and catch up after the trip. She brought along a bottle of wine and half a pan of brownies from Mildred's. Leaving the full amount in her kitchen at home would be nothing more than a reason to wear stretch pants for a week or two. Mildred's brownies were irresistible.

Riotous barking followed when she rang the doorbell. "Enough, enough, both of you." Sam was careful not to open the door too wide, allowing her to slip through before any four-legged friends got out. They were generally well-behaved, but her presence seemed to rile them up.

"Oh, no. Not the brownies. I'll have to punch a

fresh hole in all my belts." Though that didn't stop Sam from taking the plate to the kitchen.

"Excuse me. You forgot something." She caught up to him and held her arms out. He pulled her in for a hug before offering a lingering kiss that threatened to make her hair stand straight up. That was the effect he generally had on her.

"Thank you. Now that I got what I came for, I'll be leaving." She was playful, pretending to push away from his chest, but he only held on tighter than ever.

"Not a chance. And don't pretend you only came over here for a single kiss."

"Now that you mention it, there is something I thought we should discuss."

He shook his head before letting go, heading to the cabinet to pull down a pair of wine glasses. "There it is. I was waiting for it."

Normally, his sense of humor was one of the things she liked best about him. This was not a normal situation, however. "I'm serious. I've avoided bringing it up because I wasn't sure we needed to talk about it, but the more I think about it the more obvious it is. We need to talk."

Her firm tone erased what was left of the grin

still hovering around the corners of his mouth. "What's the problem?"

"I don't know that it is a problem, exactly."

"Would you get to it already?"

It all came out at once, spurred by the irritation creeping into his voice. It reminded her of Edwin, and not in a good way. "Do you have an ex-girlfriend or an ex-wife skulking around town, threatening women who seem even remotely involved with you?"

He blinked rapidly, shrinking back a bit. "Excuse me?"

"I think I was pretty clear. Do you have an ex who's capable of that? I'll describe her if it will make things easier: slim, dark-haired, blue-eyed, and probably too young for you."

His brows knitted together in what looked like a moment of embarrassment. "Oh. I see." He reached for the wine and began peeling away the foil around the cork.

She waited for more but he was too involved with the wine, so she prompted him. "Do you see? Because I don't. I'm not trying to throw old relation-ships in your face, and it's none of my business that you might have been involved with a young woman barely older than my daughter."

"Hold on a second."

She held up a hand, shaking her head. "That was unnecessary. I apologize."

"Would you stop for a minute so I can at least explain?" Yet instead of explaining straight away, he poured a glass of wine and held it out to her. He always made sure she was taken care of before taking care of himself. His thoughtfulness warmed her inside and made her regret the need for this conversation.

It did not, however, eliminate the need for it. If anything, if she wanted to enjoy his thoughtful nature—and everything else about him—they needed to start from a place of truth. No secrets, especially if those secrets might end up biting her in the backside.

"Her name is Alex. What little there was between us has been over for a long time." He stared down into his glass as if suddenly entranced by the sight of swirling merlot. "I don't know if you'll believe this, but I'll say it anyway. I tried for a very long time to stay away from her. Because you're right, she was much too young for me. But it wasn't long after the divorce and—"

"You don't have to explain anything to me. Not

that sort of thing, anyway. It's none of my business, and it was unfair of me to bring it up."

"No, you're right. I would have thought the same things if I met her without context." He started for the living room, bringing the brownies with him. This was the sort of story that required alcohol and sweets, evidently. They settled in on the sofa and he split a brownie in half before handing a piece to her.

"I was hired by Alex's mother. Back in the 90s, her husband ran a successful law firm with a business partner, and they were flying high. They decorated their offices with only the best, and that included artwork. Of course, the good times ended eventually, and with all the legal hubbub that went on once their partnership dissolved, they lost track of where the art went. It was supposed to have been held in a storage unit, at least according to Alex's mother. Her husband passed away a few years ago and reading between the lines, it became apparent she'd also run through a lot of the money he left in the will."

"Let me guess. She was hoping to sell the art to make more money."

"Naturally. She gave me this handwritten agreement, scribbled on legal paper, saying her husband was granted full ownership of the art and he could do with it whatever he wanted. So there I was, like a dog chasing its tail, trying to track down this allegedly stolen artwork. The ex-business partner moved to Arizona years ago, so I went out there to speak to him. Wouldn't you know it, a few of these so-called missing pieces were actually hanging in the house."

He shook his head, snickering before taking a bite of his brownie. It went beautifully well with the wine.

He continued, "We had a nice dinner that evening. Long story short, my client's late husband sold the art to his former partner ten years ago. The way he made it sound, the guy was already hemorrhaging money thanks to his wife's spending habits. He sold the art, evidently without telling his wife about it, to support her spending habits. He just never told her about it. When I went back to her with this information, she did everything but threaten my life."

"Oh, no."

"Well, I basically pulled the rug out from under her. There she was, believing millions of dollars' worth of art were sitting in a climate-controlled storage unit all this time. That was her big insurance policy, you know? I tried to explain things to her. I even put her in touch with the business partner with his permission. He promptly regretted that."

"I'm sure. She sounds like a real piece of work." Annie sipped her wine, wondering how to be diplomatic about what came next. "How does Alex figure into all this?"

"She was the so-called voice of reason. Rolling her eyes behind her mom's head, having private conversations with me, that sort of thing. To this day, I don't know if she was really interested in me or if her mother put her up to it. Of course, at the time it was all very flattering, you know."

He grimaced, averting his eyes when she met his gaze. "I'm not exactly proud. But like I said, I was fresh off my divorce."

"Divorce can make you do crazy things. I mean, I've heard some divorcees even move to an entirely new state to run a business they know nothing about."

He burst out laughing, which went a long way toward easing the tension in the air. "Suffice it to say, as soon as I confirmed they wouldn't be getting their hands on the art, our supposed relationship fell apart. Suddenly I was a thief. I stole what rightfully belonged to my client and her daughter. They also accused me of taking a bribe.

They tried to have me stripped of my license and everything."

"Oh, that's terrible."

"It was a lot of barking from rabid dogs. I knew they had nothing on me, no matter how many shady lawyers came out of the woodwork demanding I agree to their terms. Alex became convinced I stole her inheritance." He chuckled, rubbing his chin and wearing a wry expression. "She didn't much appreciate my pointing out her mother had done a fine job of that on her own."

"So that's what this is all about? She accuses you of stealing her inheritance?"

"That's the long and the short of it. I'm sure there were no feelings on her side. There weren't any on mine, either. But if it makes her look like more of a victim, I have no doubt she'd concoct an entire lengthy relationship I walked out on."

"Not before stealing a bunch of money from her."

"Oh, obviously." He rolled his eyes before polishing off what was left in his glass. "So now you know. That's the story."

"And she's still after you for the money?"

"I'm sure she knows by now she's not getting any money. Her mother is deluded, but Alex isn't quite that far gone. She wants to ruin my life now. And in the end, she's spoiled. Entitled."

"Well, she's going around telling people you're no good. You might want to reach out to her and, you know, threaten a restraining order or something to put a little fear in her." Then she held up her hands. "Not that it's any of my business."

"No, it's absolutely your business. She has no right to involve herself in my life in any way. How did she approach you?"

She gave him the rundown of their encounters before asking the one question that weighed heaviest on her mind. "Do you think she's unstable? I'm talking beyond spoiled and entitled. Do you think she would hurt somebody to get a point across?"

He hesitated a beat before shaking his head. "No. I don't think she would go that far."

Annie wasn't interested in what he said. What interested her most was the beat he took. He had to think about it.

"I'm sorry she's dragging you into this. She's the reason I spend my weekends here, away from work. I lost my perspective and let work and my personal life blend together. I'll never make that mistake again." He reached over, brushing his fingers over hers. "Are we okay?"

"Of course we are. What you did before we met is none of my business, and you were both adults." She bit her lip. "I hope you both were, anyway."

"Annie."

"Sorry. I had to bring it up."

"You don't know me better than that by now?"

"I do, but like I said, I know what divorce does to a person. I didn't know who I was anymore, who I wanted to be. Nothing made sense. I was lost."

"And now you're here." He laced his fingers through hers, staring at their joined hands. "I can't pretend I'm unhappy about that. You've got me spending the entire work week looking forward to being with you again. I can hardly concentrate on anything else."

"You'd better stop, or I might think you like me."

He slid across the sofa and she didn't try to stop him. Once he settled in beside her, she rested her head on his shoulder. "For what it's worth, I look forward all week to seeing you, too. The anticipation is sort of fun."

"What do you anticipate?"

She giggled, turning her face toward his neck to hide the flush on her cheeks. "What do you think?"

"Do you really want to know what I think?" He

pressed his lips against her forehead, her cheek. She turned her face toward his to meet his kiss.

"I have nowhere else to be and nothing else to do." She reached up, sliding a hand around the back of his neck and running her fingers through his hair while he kissed her again.

"I think it's about time…" Another kiss, then another. "… you spend the night with me."

Heat unfurled low in her belly and began to spread through her. "I've already spent the night with you. Remember?"

"I was thinking more along the lines of our sharing my bed this time, rather than one of us sleeping out here."

Her heart fluttered and breath caught in her throat when his lips skimmed that particular body part. Her skin fairly sizzled but she wouldn't have tried to stop him for anything in the world. Not when there was an inferno threatening to burst to life deep inside her. "It's a very comfortable bed, if I remember correctly."

"It certainly is." He nipped her earlobe before going in for another, deeper kiss. If she'd possessed even a shred of doubt, that shred would have burned to ash in the heat from what he was doing to her.

By the time she came up for air, there wasn't a

doubt in her mind. "I think I could spend a night away from home, now that you mention it."

"Good." He kissed the tip of her nose before looking deep into her eyes. "Because the other side of the bed is sure lonely without you."

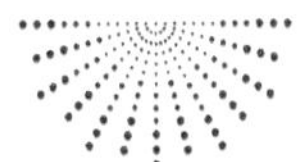

And so, they were on the road again.

It was different this time, and not only because they weren't flying. This time, instead of taking a trip into the unknown, Annie knew very well what they would find once they reached New Jersey.

And it had her stomach in knots.

That was silly, and she knew it was silly. What did she expect? For Edwin to pop up out of nowhere? To run into every gossiping, negative person from the past? Maybe an old boyfriend would show up out of nowhere, or the ghost of her mother. There was no reason for her anxiety to run so high, yet she was still as jittery as she'd be after a third cup of coffee.

Tyler's anxiety gave her something to focus on in a desperate attempt to distract herself. "Don't be so nervous. You have nothing to be worried about."

"Who said I was nervous?"

"You don't have to say it. The fact that you haven't stopped cracking your knuckles since we rolled into Virginia tells me everything I need to know."

"Sometimes they need to be cracked."

"I know you do that when you're feeling stressed." She glanced at him from the corner of her eye and found him scowling. "I'm trying to tell you you don't have any reason to be."

"I don't know why I am. She's just a kid."

"Yes, she is. Be sure not to call her one, though. Not if you want to be able to swallow food, since she'll probably punch you in the throat."

"Noted." At least he laughed, and she joined him.

They had just crossed the Delaware River and were in southern New Jersey with more than two hours left in the drive when he asked if they could pull in at the next rest stop. Annie was more than glad to do it, since she, too, needed a break. The moment she opened the car door, she smiled to herself.

Tyler, however, wasn't smiling. "What's that

smell?" He sniffed the air, frowning at her from over the roof of the car.

"It could be all the exhaust fumes from the trucks parked yonder." She gestured to the area where a row of enormous trucks sat.

"No, that's not what I'm smelling."

"Then it could be New Jersey itself. Come on, fill your lungs." She inhaled deeply, laughing when he pretended to gag. "Come on. We're practically next to the river, for heaven's sake. Do you expect to smell roses?"

"No, but I hope to smell something that doesn't make me want to throw up."

"Then maybe I'd better cart you back over the bridge to Delaware." He made a sour face but dropped the subject on their way into the squat, long building. It was packed, so much so that there was a line for the ladies' room. It seemed plenty of people were able to get the entire week off for the holiday and were trying to get a jump on their travel.

She sent Melanie a text while waiting. *Looks like we'll be there in plenty of time. Going to drop our things off at the motel before heading over to the restaurant.*

By the time she finished in the bathroom, there was a message waiting for her. *What time is the reservation again?*

All it would have taken was a quick scroll through their previous string of messages. Melanie was normally on top of things, sometimes alarmingly so. Type-A, all the way. And yet. *7:00. Do you need us to pick you up at the train station?*

"Is everything okay?"

Annie jumped, startled at what seemed to her like Tyler's sudden appearance. "Oh, sure. Texting Mel." As an afterthought, she added another message. *Don't forget to pack a bag for the night. You have no idea how much I'm looking forward to spending time with you.* She smiled when she sent it, because it was true. It had been too long since they'd spent any meaningful time together aside from phone calls.

"You weren't kidding about it being cold up here." Tyler zipped his jacket and shivered on the way to the car.

"See? And you didn't want to bring a jacket at all."

"You don't have to rub it in." Granted, it got cool in North Carolina, but nothing like the nip in the air now. She took a deep breath, welcoming the bracing air and even the smell from the river. It reminded her of home, of trips to the beach, of all the things she'd enjoyed during what she'd believed were the good days.

Before moving on, she checked the phone one

more time. Melanie had responded. *I'll just get an Uber from the station. See you there.* That was it. Nothing about the motel or looking forward to hanging out. Annie's chest tightened. What wasn't her daughter telling her?

"Are you okay?" Tyler would never point out the obvious, that she was as worried about Melanie as he was—if for different reasons. Still, his question reminded Annie to lighten her mood for his sake.

"Fine. Overthinking, as usual." She tucked the phone into the console and started the car. Reading too much into the emotional ups and downs of a young woman was the surest route to madness. Whatever was bothering Melanie would pass by evening.

She needed to believe that.

~

*I*t was cold. Truly, deeply cold. And thanks to the fact that she'd been in North Carolina for months, her body hadn't had the chance to acclimate. She pulled up her collar and wrapped the coat tighter around her, rocking back and forth from her heels to the balls of her feet while waiting on Melanie's Uber. Tyler waited inside—not because he couldn't stand the cold, but because he wanted to be sure their table wasn't given away. It was already ten minutes past seven, and the hostess had looked frazzled enough when they'd arrived well before their reservation time.

Annie was about to send Melanie another text when a black sedan pulled to a stop in front of the restaurant. She waited, her heart in her throat, then almost collapsed in relief when Melanie unfolded herself from the back seat.

She looked older. More mature.

And weary. When Annie rushed over, arms outstretched, Melanie shrank back for a moment before accepting the hug her mother so eagerly offered. "Sorry, it took longer than I thought to get a car."

"No worries. So long as you're here." Annie held her at arm's length, beaming. "You look fantastic. A little too thin, maybe."

Melanie grinned, rolling her eyes. "I'm not too thin. I'm the same weight I was the last time you saw me."

"And you were too thin then, too." Annie hugged her again, closing her eyes and breathing in her baby's scent. Not the same as it was when she was an infant, but there was still something inherently, uniquely Melanie about her. And it had been too long since Annie had been able to revel in her.

"Come on." She wound an arm around her daughter's waist. "We better get inside before they give our table away. Tyler has been making sure the hostess knows we're still here."

Melanie's stride faltered. "He's here?"

"Of course, I told you he was coming with me. After all the talking I do about you, I'm sure he's looking forward to finally meeting face-to-face."

"I'm looking forward to meeting him, too." Only there was nothing friendly or lighthearted or even pleasant about the expression Melanie wore as they walked into the restaurant. Annie's observational skills kicked into overdrive. This wasn't her imagination. Something was wrong.

For the sake of everybody, she put on her happiest face before waving at Tyler, then working her way through the crowd waiting to be seated. "Here she is! Melanie, meet Tyler. Tyler, this is my daughter."

Despite his nerves, he smiled warmly. It still amazed Annie how his smile transformed his face. He looked younger, not to mention handsome, as he extended a hand. "It's nice to finally meet you. I'm pretty sure I know your entire life story already."

Melanie mustered a grin. "I shudder to think."

"Now he can get information straight from the source, right?" Annie's smile felt brittle, too bright. She was already trying too hard to compensate for the discomfort, which naturally made things more awkward.

Was this a mistake? They had yet to sit down and order appetizers, but Annie was beginning to think it was. The hostess grabbed three menus and motioned for them to follow her to a table. Tyler took the lead, with Annie and Melanie following.

Annie grabbed Melanie's arm. "Are you okay? Do you not feel well?"

"I'm fine."

It wasn't until then that Annie realized what was missing. "You don't have a bag with you. Remember, I got us that room for the night."

"Oh. I guess I forgot to bring it." They reached the table and took their seats, with Melanie sitting opposite Tyler and Annie sitting between them.

"Well, you know me. I always pack a few extra things just in case. I could give you a nightshirt."

"Whatever, it's fine. Maybe I'll just Uber back to the train after."

Annie leaned over, lowering her voice. "I told you what the plan was. Why are you acting like this?"

"Good evening, everybody." The chipper server joined them, standing behind the empty fourth chair. "I would love to tell you about our specials this evening, but first, can I get you all something to drink?"

"I'll have an iced tea." Tyler offered a tight smile, but the strain was clear. He was no fool. He saw there was something wrong.

"I'll have the same." Annie looked at Melanie, who shrugged. "I guess that makes three."

"Great. I'll be right back with those, and we'll look into those specials." It was almost a relief when the girl left. She seemed sweet enough, but Annie's hopes for the evening were already circling the drain. It almost took too much effort to be pleasant.

Don't push. Don't push. She gritted her teeth against the impulse to demand her daughter open up. "Should we maybe have rescheduled this? I know you're coming up on the end of the semester in a couple of weeks. Are we keeping you from studying?"

"No, it's fine. I'm just tired." Melanie gazed across the table at Tyler. "How are we related again? I'm still not totally clear on that."

Annie bit back a harsh comment. The question hadn't been directed at her, after all.

"It's sort of a long story. How much has your mother told you?" Tyler slid an almost panicked look in Annie's direction.

"But I want to hear it from you. First, she told me you guys were brother and sister, but then she said you're not."

Annie barely stopped short of kicking Melanie under the table. "Excuse me. Don't talk about me like I'm not here. You're being rude."

Tyler cleared his throat. "As it turns out, we're cousins."

"Do we really have to talk about this in the restaurant?" Annie forced a brittle smile. "This is something we could have discussed over the phone if you were that curious."

Melanie folded her arms. Suddenly she was twelve again, going through puberty mood swings. "We could have, but we didn't, did we? Sorry if I want to know who my mother is living with hundreds of miles away."

Tyler was full of surprises. Instead of closing up, shutting down the way he might have when he and Annie first met, he leaned in slightly, folding his arms on the table. "As it turns out, the man you thought was your grandfather was not. I know you never met him, and trust me, you're not missing anything. But he was my father, and he's a real piece of work."

He jerked a thumb in Annie's direction. "He was such a terrible husband, your grandmother took up with his brother. *He* is your grandfather."

Melanie blew out a sigh through pursed lips. "What a family. Good to know who I come from."

This time, Annie did nudge her ankle. "Last time I checked, you have nothing to complain about. I don't appreciate this attitude. You asked a question, Tyler answered."

"Let's be frank. I know you don't like the idea of me." Tyler shrugged. "And I came here anyway because I knew how you were probably feeling. I figured maybe talking like this, over dinner, you'd eventually feel a little better."

The server came back with their drinks, and she couldn't have come at a better time in Annie's opinion. Her face was so hot, her embarrassment so acute. Sure, Melanie was grown, but there would never come a time she wouldn't feel responsible for the things her daughter did. She would never stop feeling like it reflected on her as a mother.

"I'm sorry. We haven't even looked at the menu yet." Annie opened hers and quickly skimmed.

"No worries. Take your time. I'll grab some bread

for the table, and when I come back, I'll be happy to answer any questions you have." Annie almost wanted to ask if she could go along with the girl if only to escape this impossible situation.

"Is there anything else you want to know?" Tyler took a long sip of his tea. Annie wanted desperately to apologize but held her tongue. This was their problem, not hers. Some things she couldn't get in the middle of.

"Why are you living with my mom? Why don't you have a place of your own? What do you want from her?"

"I don't want anything from her. As for where I live, your mother offered me a spare room. I wouldn't have asked for it. I was already renting a place. But after she went through all that trouble when she first moved to town, it made her feel better to have someone else in the house."

Annie jumped in, nodding her head. "I've already told you all of this." To think, she'd been looking forward to spending time with her daughter. How blind could she have been? Clearly there was a great deal of resentment and suspicion on Melanie's part.

Tyler waved it off. "Don't worry about it. Like I said, I knew Melanie would have questions. I knew she might even resent me being around. The only thing I can say is, your mother is a good woman. She likes to take care of people, and for some reason, she thinks I'm worthy of that. But I don't want anything from her. I'm not trying to scam her or anything like that. You don't have to worry about her."

Melanie nodded but said nothing. Annie shot Tyler an apologetic look, but he appeared to brush it off. Maybe he truly was accustomed to this sort of suspicion. That didn't make it right, though.

Once they finally got their food, it looked delicious and smelled just as good, but Annie barely tasted a bite of it. She was too busy trying to pick up the mood around the table. She asked Melanie about her classes, about her friends, then finally got around to a subject she'd turned over in her head a few times but had not yet mentioned.

"You know, I'm breaking my brain trying to come up with ways to bring more customers into the store." She speared a piece of chicken, glancing up at her daughter as if this was nothing more than a casual thought and not a desperate attempt to include her. "I was thinking about doing more work on social media for advertising."

Melanie nodded. "Yeah, it's kind of a no-brainer. That's what everybody does now."

"But the thing is, I don't know the first thing about that."

Melanie snorted. "I know."

"But you do, right? You're all over Facebook and the... what's it called? Insta-something?"

"Instagram. Yes, that, too."

"Right. So I was wondering, could you help me with that? I couldn't afford to pay you much at first, but I would like to throw a little something your way."

Melanie's brows drew together. "I would never charge you."

"I don't expect you to do it for free. And I wouldn't want it to get in the way of your school-work. That's most important."

"I could get started over break. Schedule a bunch of content in advance." There was even a little bit of excitement in her voice, which brought Annie no small measure of relief.

Even so, there was noticeable awkwardness at the table through the rest of the meal. Annie kept reminding herself not to apologize for Melanie's sullen disposition. It wasn't easy, especially when she knew it had to bother Tyler. He handled it well, but she recognized by now what it looked like when his defenses came up. Something about the set of his jaw, even the way he held his knife and fork. He was braced for the next attack, on the alert.

Which was why Annie pulled Melanie aside on the way out of the restaurant. They'd decided against dessert in an attempt at bringing the evening to an end before any blood was shed. "Whether you like it or not, you're coming to the motel. We need to have a talk."

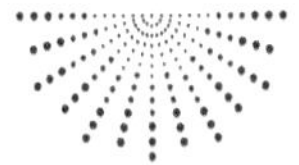

CHAPTER EIGHT

"No offense, but maybe I should just get on the train and head back up."

Annie threw a look over her shoulder to where Melanie stood in the doorway to the room. "Would you mind closing that? It's November, in case nobody told you." She intended for the quip to come out like a joke, lighthearted, yet even to her ears, it sounded harsh and nagging.

"Which side of the door do you want me to be on?"

"Inside the room, which I'm sure you know very well." Annie dropped her purse on the dresser before sitting at the foot of one of the twin beds, shrugging helplessly. "What did I do? What's changed? I know you've been mad at me for a long time—"

"No, don't say that." Melanie's body language told another story, however. Her shoulders were up around her ears, her arms folded over her midsection.

Annie deliberately softened her tone in hopes of easing the tension. "But you have been. You don't have to worry about hurting my feelings or causing some huge rift between us. Get that out of your mind now. Nothing you say to me will ever break our relationship permanently. We're not going to let that happen. I'm your mother, and I will always love you."

She drew a deep breath, forcing herself to say the rest before she lost her nerve. "But right now, after the performance you gave at the restaurant, I'm not sure I like you very much."

Melanie paled. "That's a nice thing to say."

"I'm sorry, but did they not teach you yet at NYU that you shouldn't expect kindness and mercy if you aren't willing to give either?" Annie folded her arms to match her daughter's posture. "No, on second thought. I taught you that. You were raised better than this. Has your time in college made you forget?"

"Could you not make it about that?"

"Could you tell me where this unkind attitude comes from?"

"When have I ever been unkind to you?"

"I'm not talking about myself. I'm talking about Tyler, and you know it."

The eye roll was epic. "Of course you are. You're always talking about Tyler. What Tyler needs, how well Tyler is doing."

"Is that the problem? Do you resent him? I thought you didn't trust him, but I didn't realize it ran that deep."

Melanie sat on the other bed, but just barely. As if she was still on the fence over whether she would stay. "I don't know how I feel."

"Let's talk about it."

"Would it make a difference?"

"It would to me. And if it's going to help you, then of course. I want to understand where you're coming from."

So much had changed over the years as her daughter had matured. Melanie had gone from a precocious little girl to a bright, but shy, teenager. Always smart, always levelheaded—but like all kids, she possessed doubt, especially when it came to voicing opinions that might run counter to those of a trusted adult.

Now she was a headstrong young woman, but she still had those same little tells. Like now, when she ducked her head and tucked her hair behind her ears. She had run her mouth and now wondered if she had maybe said too much. "It's just really weird for me. Hearing about this whole other life you have now. I don't like it."

"Do you want to feel like you're more a part of it?"

"I don't know what I want. But I know I don't totally trust some random stranger living with you. It makes me feel uncomfortable." She let out a shaky breath. "Dad, too."

Annie bit back a sharp rebuke. Barely. "What does your father have to do with any of this?"

"Obviously, he asks about you sometimes."

"I didn't think I needed to say it out loud, but perhaps I do. Look at me." Melanie lifted her eyes, clearly reluctant. "My personal life and my choices are none of his business. Our marriage is over. We share you, of course, but that's it."

"So you expect him to stop caring?"

Annie squeezed her eyes shut, gritting her teeth. *She thinks she's doing the right thing. This is coming from a good place.* "I need you to respect my feelings on this, Melanie."

"You can't pretend you were never married when you were the one—"

"Don't." Annie's eyes popped open, and now she couldn't hold back her growing irritation. "Don't put the blame on me. I know that's what you've always done. You were always daddy's girl, so I've brushed it off as best I could."

"You don't have to be insulting about it."

"I wasn't trying to be. I was stating a fact. You've consistently taken his side when none of what I did would've been necessary if he'd avoided cheating on me in the first place. Years of lying, making me feel like I was crazy for doubting him. In the end, I was right all along."

"But you spied on him."

"I did. And I regret that now, though I wouldn't change the outcome." Melanie gasped, which only hardened her mother's resolve. "Would you rather I continue being disrespected? Would that make you feel better? Mom can wait faithfully at home for her husband to show up after visiting his girlfriend, so long as your perfect family unit remains intact?"

Melanie winced. "No. Of course not."

"He was never going to come out with the truth so long as he was happy and content with the way things were, honey. He needed to be found out. And I don't regret the outcome, as I said. At least now I can respect myself."

"He's still your ex-husband, and he still cares about you. Why can't I answer questions if he asks?"

"Does he ask a lot of questions?"

"He always asks how you're doing. He's concerned."

The folly of youth. While Annie believed Edwin still cared at least a little—just as she did for him, despite everything—she possessed deeper insight into the lingering emotions left behind post-divorce. On top of that, Melanie saw her father as just that. Her father. She didn't have the first idea what it meant to know the man and how insidious and judgmental his so-called concern and advice could be.

Rather than go into it, Annie spared her. "My life is my life. He chose to cut himself out of it when he chose to break his vows. I don't need to explain myself further."

"See? That's exactly what I'm talking about."

"What is exactly what you're talking about? I'm entitled to have a life of my own. to make choices of my own. I'm a grown woman. I appreciate your caring, but I think you're losing sight of the fact that I am your mother. You are my daughter. You don't call the shots for me."

She expected an apology after that small rant or

at least a promise her daughter would respect her wishes. Instead, Melanie twisted her lips in an achingly familiar moue of disapproval. "You've changed."

Annie's mouth fell open—then snapped shut just as suddenly. It was the truth of her daughter's statement that stole her voice. She had changed. She was different. "I know I have. You're right. I'm not the same person I was before the divorce or even before I moved."

"At least you see it." Melanie studied the bedspread, picking at a loose thread like it was the most important thing in the world.

Annie scooted closer to her, swinging her legs around so she was facing her daughter. "Is that such a bad thing? I haven't changed who I am inside. Not the real me. I'm still your mom, and I still love you just the way I always have."

"I know that." Melanie glanced up before averting her gaze again. "But, you know, you're still different. You do things you never would have done before. You never trusted strangers. You didn't do crazy things like having some random person move in with you. And if you didn't want me to be worried about his past, you shouldn't have told me about it."

"You're right about that. I shouldn't have told

you, but not for the reason you think. Tyler's life is Tyler's life. His choices were his, no one else's. And until you've walked a mile in his shoes, to use an adage, you have no room to criticize. Neither do I."

When Melanie snickered softly, she came dangerously close to losing her patience. "That much hasn't changed. That much, I know I taught you. Understanding. Forgiveness. Because I'll tell you something, young lady. From where I'm sitting, you've become a person I don't recognize very easily, and I don't like it, either. But I'm sure you have your reasons, right?"

"I haven't changed."

"That's not true. You're defending your close-mindedness, cloaking it under concern for me. And I understand. I truly do. I guess I was naive hoping you would feel better once you got to know him a little bit. This trip was supposed to ease your concerns. Because once you get to know him, you'll see he's just like you or me. Only he got dealt a much worse hand and either of us did."

Melanie rolled her eyes. "You didn't have it so easy."

"No, I didn't, but I still had it better than him. He lost his adoptive parents when he was still a teenager. Can you imagine if you'd lost me and your dad when you were that young? He had no other family, and nowhere to go. He did what he had to do to survive. We've both been much luckier than he was."

Melanie chewed her lip, her brow furrowed. "I didn't know that."

"No, you didn't, but you could have. I'm sure he would have shared that with you if you'd even thought to ask how he grew up, what he liked to do. Anything to treat him as a human being who happens to share a little bit of DNA with you. But instead, you judged him, and you used me as an excuse to do it."

"I'm just worried about you." Melanie's voice wavered like she was on the verge of tears. "I don't know anything about you anymore. And I'm so scared I'm going to get a call that something really bad happened and this time you didn't get so lucky." she covered her face with her hands, but that wasn't enough to completely muffle a broken sob.

Annie's heart lurched. She moved to the other bed and enfolded her daughter in her arms. "I'm sorry. I'm never meant to scare you or make you worry about me. It kills me to think I caused you to feel this way."

"It's not your fault."

It was habit, rocking her when she was upset. Annie fell into a slow rhythm, stroking her daughter's hair. "I can't have you worrying about me. My life is mine to live. I don't know who gave you the idea I needed looking after, but that's just not true. I've had some sticky situations, but I've come out even better on the other side."

Melanie nodded, wiping her eyes with the heels of her hands. "It's a lot to adjust to."

"You wouldn't have lived with me once school started anyway, right?"

"But if you were, like, still in Jersey and living the way you used to, it would be different."

"I'm sorry to tell you, but that's just not how things are. And they never will be again." Annie took her by the chin, lifting her head slightly so they could meet eye to eye. "But I won't apologize for building a life of my own. I needed to do that, and I'm glad I did. I only wish it didn't hurt you."

Melanie narrowed her eyes. "So you're really happy the way you're living right now?"

Rather than deliver a quick response, she thought it over. Was she happy? She had the store. She had Mildred's friendship. She had the house and Sam and Tyler and Bogart. It was a simple life that would never warrant a grand biopic.

It was hers, though. She was building something she was proud of. Something that belonged to her, not to a husband who could easily take everything away because he was going through a midlife crisis.

"I am happy. And I'm proud of myself." She lifted her chin, pulling a smug expression in hopes Melanie would laugh. "It took guts, moving to a totally new place."

"It did." Melanie mustered a brief smile. "It was brave, doing that."

"You have no idea how nice it is to hear you say that." Annie kissed her forehead before hugging her again. "That doesn't mean I'm moving on from you. You have to know you're still the center of my world. And I'm proud of you. But I kind of like being proud of myself, too. A funny thing to learn in your old age."

Melanie pulled her head back and treated her mother to a withering look. "You're not old."

"Tell that to my back when I've been standing behind the counter at the store for too long." She laughed off Melanie's eye roll. "You'll figure it out one day."

"Now I feel really bad about the way I was at dinner. Did I really hurt Tyler's feelings?"

"You could hold his feet over a fire and he would

never admit it, but I'm pretty sure you must have. He didn't expect you to welcome him with open arms, but I think he was still wounded by the way you were acting."

Melanie hopped up off the bed and marched to the little bathroom. "I have to go apologize."

"I'm sure it could wait until morning."

"No, it can't. I'll never be able to get to sleep until I make things right." Melanie finished washing her face and quickly dried it on a hand towel. "I feel terrible for acting like I did. Do you think he'll forgive me?"

"He's a forgiving person. Surprisingly even-tempered considering where he's come from." And who. It would be better to leave that part out. As much as Annie didn't want any more secrets, until things were settled with Gavin it would be better to leave their respective fathers out of it.

"Mom." Melanie paused at the foot of the bed, biting her lip again. She looked so touchingly young, unsure of herself. "I'm sorry. I don't want you thinking it's wrong to have your own life or what-ever. That's not what I think. I think it's brave, what you did. I just hate that I can't swing by and check in on you."

"It should be the other way around, remember?"

Melanie shuffled her feet, hunching her shoulders, and Annie took pity on her. "You've always been too old for your years. I don't want you thinking you ever have to watch over me, but I appreciate you wanting to. Lots of parents lose their kids once they start college. I don't want that for us."

"Neither do I." Melanie bent down to give her mother a fierce hug before untangling herself and going to the door. "Okay. I have to do a little groveling."

Were this any other circumstance, she might assure Melanie there was nothing to grovel about if only to ease her apprehension. But that wouldn't do anyone any favors. Besides, if she wanted to be a grown-up, the kid had to learn to own her actions.

Still, Annie waited until the door closed to tiptoe over and open it a crack so she might hear a little of what was going on outside the room next door.

The door opened, and Melanie was the first to speak. "I owe you an apology for how I acted. I understand if you don't want to hear it and wouldn't blame you if you close the door in my face, but I at least wanted you to know I'm sorry and I wish I could take it back."

There was a moment of silence before the door creaked.

"Come on in."

Annie smiled in relief before closing her own door as quietly as she could.

It was starting to look like this trip wasn't such a waste of time, after all.

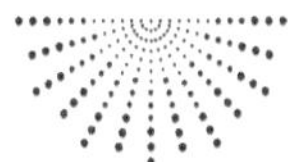

CHAPTER NINE

"By breakfast the next morning, everything was fine. They chatted like two old friends." Annie finished pulling the last of the foil containers from the oven, where Mildred had placed them to stay warm after delivery.

"I wonder what they talked about in his room?"

"I didn't want to pry, so I didn't ask. Whatever it was, it did the trick."

"No, dear. You did the trick by telling your daughter exactly what she needed to hear." Mildred peered at Annie from over the rims of her spectacles. "And what you needed to get off your chest, it seems."

"I guess you're right about that."

"And did you feel better once you spoke your mind?"

"Quite a lot."

"There you go. I'm proud of you." Mildred scowled when Annie merely laughed it off. "It's true. I'm proud of you for taking a stand. Children are wonderful, but they have a tendency to think they know everything. I can't tell you how many serious chats I had with my students back when I was teaching."

She chuckled, and it was the sound of a woman with a great many memories behind her. "There's nothing like the confidence of a child who really knows nothing."

Annie chuckled over that herself. "I shouldn't laugh. I was the same way."

"We all were. That's why adults see it so much more clearly than children do, because we've all been there."

"Yes, and I remember how resentful I was whenever my mother knew better than I did. That's why I'm hesitant to be too hard on Melanie. I don't want her thinking she can't come to me when she has a problem because I'll hold it over her head that I knew better than she did."

"Is that what your mother did to you?"

"No comment." They exchanged a look, both of them smirking a bit.

"To be fair, your mother didn't have a very easy time of it. I'm sure she didn't want you to go through any of the same things she did."

"You have a point. I certainly know a lot more of the story now."

Mildred wiped her hands on her apron, sighing as she looked over the array of dishes. "I hope the boys don't mind a store-bought meal for Thanksgiving."

"Are you kidding? This looks and smells amazing. It doesn't matter who cooked it—though I do wish you had let me take care of it."

"Nonsense. You work hard enough as it is. You don't need to break your back making Thanksgiving dinner on top of everything else." Mildred's lips twitched. "Besides, you know how fond I am of you, but no one touches my kitchen."

Yes, and she wouldn't leave the house. Annie wondered silently if Mildred's agoraphobia was permanent. She'd started walking around the garden outside the house, which according to her was a great improvement over barely being able to fetch the mail without suffering heart palpitations. Asking her to come over for Thanksgiving dinner had been completely off the table, so they'd compromised with a catered meal.

Mildred's beautiful china gleamed once Annie lit the candles in the dining room. The sounds of a football game drifted in from the parlor, where Sam and Tyler sat in what she hoped was companionable silence. They didn't exactly get along, but at least they'd been civil so far. If Melanie could come around, maybe Sam could, too.

"We could use a little help getting the food on the table." Moments later, she heard the men getting up from their chairs. It sounded like they were discussing the game, which gave her hope. It mattered so much that the people in her life got along, maybe too much. That had always been a problem of hers, something Edwin used to tease her about in the early days of their relationship. The way she took it upon herself to be the mother hen of whatever group she was part of.

"Mildred, this is too much. You shouldn't have gone to all this trouble, ordering so much food for just the four of us." Sam grabbed the bowl of mashed potatoes and the candied yams while Tyler picked up green beans and cornbread dressing.

Mildred waved a hand at Sam's admonishment. "That's what this holiday is about. Abundance. And

I'm too happy to have all of you here to care very much about whether or not there's too much food."

"Make sure you save room for dessert." That had been Annie's job, so she and Tyler had arrived armed with three pies: pumpkin, apple, and pecan. Tyler had teased her endlessly over making three pies for only four people, but she shared Mildred's sensibility when it came to the holidays. Why not go overboard whenever possible?

Granted, if she wasn't careful she would need to stick to stretch pants for a while. The sight of so much food alone caused her waistband to feel a little snug as she set down the platter of turkey in the center of the table.

Once they were seated, Mildred led them in a brief blessing. "I'm so thankful to have friends here with me today. I can't tell you what a blessing it is to know all of you. You've given me a new lease on life, since for a while there, I asked myself what purpose there was in living any longer. I thought my life was over. Now I see it was just the end of a chapter. And I hope there are many more chapters and many more holidays like this one."

Annie reached over and touched her friend's hand, fighting back tears. "I feel the same way. I never thought when I took over the store that I would inherit a dear friend in the process." She then looked at Tyler. "And you might not be my brother, but you feel like one."

Sam cleared his throat. "And?"

Annie narrowed her eyes but was unable to fight back a smile. "No comment."

He put a hand to his chest like he was wounded, which Mildred got a big kick out of. Even Tyler almost grinned before they started tearing into the food.

As they loaded their plates, Mildred mused aloud. "You know, I've never been one of those people who believes much in that so-called nuclear family nonsense. Don't misunderstand me. Family is a wonderful thing, but it doesn't need to strictly be limited to blood relations. Sometimes, we aren't fortunate enough for our blood relations to pan out the way we'd like them to."

Tyler let out a knowing laugh. "Isn't that the truth."

Mildred continued, "There's nothing we can do to change that. I've gone through it with my own blood relations. It's been a long time, but that's not the sort of thing a person forgets easily. The sense that you aren't understood by the people you want most to understand you. Or worse, that they don't accept you. I've been through that, too."

"There's something to be said for found family." Sam winked at her from across the table.

Clearly, Mildred was undaunted. "That's precisely what I'm getting at. Family doesn't need to be defined strictly by blood. What matters is having people around you who will go to bat for you when it counts. We will look in on you and make sure you're doing alright. Who will go out of their way to help you, even if you don't want to admit you need the help."

"Why do I get the feeling you're directing this my way?" Tyler looked and sounded like he was joking, but Annie knew there was always a kernel of truth at the center of every joke. He didn't like being the center of attention, especially in front of Sam.

Mildred shrugged it off. "Was I talking about you? I thought I was talking about myself." Annie pressed her lips together tight, ducking her head to hide her grin.

Mildred was unstoppable. "Though now that you mention it, I suppose my ramblings could apply to you as well. It doesn't matter who you came from or where. It doesn't even have to matter that a person made reckless choices in the past. What matters is finding good people and surrounding yourself with them. Building a family for yourself whether or not they're related by blood. I feel just as strongly for Annie and you as I would if you were my children. That's how much you've come to mean." She winked at Sam. "No offense, but I don't know you well enough yet."

"None taken."

"Only we can decide what our lives will become. And from what I've seen, both of you have done a mighty fine job of making the best of a poor situation. Annie, you're a businesswoman. Tyler, you're well on the way to a successful business yourself. Every time I see one of the neighbors outside, they comment on how wonderful the roof looks. I spend so much time singing your praises I've considered asking for a finder's fee from now on."

He mustered a self-conscious smile. "You would deserve it, too."

"As if I would ever accept it. Or if I did, I would put it in an account in your name."

Annie could no longer fight off laughter. "Give it up. You know she's always going to have the last word."

A buzzing sound drew their attention. Sam

checked his phone, his eyebrows shooting up. "Dallas got another touchdown going into halftime."

"Of course they did." Tyler rolled his eyes.

"Excuse me, but we don't use our phones at the Thanksgiving dinner table." Annie wagged a finger in Sam's direction. "I turned mine off because I'm not rude like some people."

"Sorry, Mom."

She stuck her tongue out at him, but at least he turned off the phone before sliding it back into his pocket.

"Those phones. All this technology. I swear, I will never understand it. We used to live just fine back in the day without gadgets weighing us down all the time." Mildred mimicked Annie's finger wag. "Besides, that thing could be giving you cancer for all you know."

"Oh, please, don't tell me that." Annie put a hand over her heart. "If I didn't have my phone on me, I would never get in touch with my kid, for starters."

"Admit it." Tyler turned toward Mildred. "How much easier has it made things? Back in the day, if you were stranded in the middle of nowhere, you had no hope of getting help unless a car drove by. And then, you were lucky if the driver was a decent person and not some maniac."

"I suppose that's true, but there's a world of difference between using the phone as a tool and being glued to it all the time." Nobody could argue with that, so they didn't bother.

They spent the rest of the meal talking about other things, including the upcoming holidays and how they hoped to spend them. "I was thinking of having a little Christmas dinner at the house." Annie looked to Tyler, brows lifted in a silent request for feedback. They hadn't discussed it yet, probably because she hadn't given the idea much serious thought until then. It felt right, sitting together like a family. She wanted to keep the feeling alive.

Mildred pressed her lips into a thin line and stared down at her plate. Annie slowly, carefully cut into a slice of turkey. "Anyone who feels they're able to make it is welcome. But there's no pressure." A stolen glance at Mildred told her she was no less troubled.

"Will Melanie come down for that?"

Annie grinned at Tyler. "You tell me. The two of you are best friends after the trip."

"Better question: do you think your ex would be okay with it?"

Annie frowned at Sam's perfectly reasonable question. "I guess we'll have to talk it over. I would like to be able to spend a holiday with my daughter. In the end, it's entirely up to her, what she feels like doing. But if I find out he's trying to influence her, he's going to have to deal with me."

"My, my, my. The energy around this table has gotten far too tense." Mildred waved her napkin as if it were a fan and she was cooling herself off. "I can barely catch my breath."

"I'm sorry." The fact was, in the days since her talk with Melanie, Annie's opinion of Edwin had sunk even lower than before. She couldn't have imagined it before then, since she hadn't thought highly of him to begin with. The man insisted on finding ways to surprise her.

Eventually, they would need to have it out. She wasn't about to let him control her life through their daughter. She'd told herself to wait until after Melanie had returned to school post-Thanksgiving break so he wouldn't give their daughter grief while they were under the same roof.

Besides, it would be wise to wait until her anger cooled. There was no telling what she'd hurl at him if she went into a conversation still holding anger. Considering the bitterness still bubbling in her chest, it looked like she might have to wait until Easter.

"I meant what I said about Christmas." Annie shifted the leftover containers from one arm to the other so she could take Mildred's hand before leaving. "There's no pressure, but it would be so lovely to have you there for even a little while. We could arrange to have you brought over to the house. Sam or Tyler would be happy to come over and pick you up, I'm sure."

Mildred patted her hand, wearing a sad little smile. "I'll think about it. But I can't make any promises."

"I understand." She pressed a kiss against the older woman's soft cheek before stepping out into the cool night. Tyler had already packed additional leftovers into the back seat—Mildred had insisted, and had done the same with Sam. He had agreed to stop by Annie's for an extra cup of coffee and what he'd almost reverently referred to as Second Desert which, according to him, was the best part of any holiday feast.

"So you two seemed to get along pretty well." Annie glanced at Tyler as she buckled her seat belt. "That was nice to see."

"He's not a bad guy, but don't make a big deal about it."

"I won't." She made a mental note to tamp down her enthusiasm.

Despite the pleasant day they'd spent, he was brooding. Annie could almost feel it coming from his side of the car as she drove home. "After cleaning everything up, I'm almost as tired now as I would have been if I'd made dinner." Why she felt the need to keep talking, she didn't know. It was better than sitting in silence, wondering what he was thinking.

Finally, he clued her in. "What was all that talk about found family? I didn't like feeling like I was being patronized."

"No one is trying to patronize you. That much, I can tell you with confidence."

"Are you a mindreader all of a sudden?"

"No, but I like to think I know Mildred well enough by now to know for sure she would never do that. She's a straight shooter, all the way."

He grumbled but relented. "That's true."

"And she likes you a lot. She sees something in you. That's important."

"I'm nobody's charity case."

"She knows that, and so do I." She patted his arm and was glad when he didn't pull it away. "But she made a good point, and you weren't the only person she was speaking to. I found a new sort of family out here, too. I sort of wish Melanie could have heard it. She might understand a little better."

They hadn't spoken much about his conversation with Melanie, mostly because he tended to shut down Annie's attempts. This time, he didn't try so hard. "Really, she's concerned about you. At the end of the day, that's where her attitude comes from. She's worried about her mom."

"You can't understand how that makes me feel as a mother. Like I'm failing somehow because my child has to worry about me instead of it being the other way around."

"Take it easy on yourself."

"As long as you promise to take it easier on yourself. Meaning you don't beat yourself up anymore for where you came from or what you had to do to live."

He snorted. "You're good at that. Finding a way to turn things around so I'm in the hot seat."

She chose to ignore the comment. "I'm waiting for your promise."

"How about I say I'll do my best?"

"I can live with that." She was smiling as she turned into the driveway, and her smile widened when Sam pulled up at the curb a few moments later. Tyler kept his thoughts on the visit to himself, instead taking the leftovers inside and placing them in the fridge while Annie waited for Sam at the front door.

"Is your phone still off? I tried to call to see if you wanted me to stop off at my place first to grab something to add to our coffee. I was thinking Baileys, maybe."

Annie groaned, slapping a palm to her forehead. So much for bragging about turning her phone off for dinner. "It's alright. I would've told you not to bother stopping off." She went to the kitchen to put on a pot of coffee while powering her phone up, humming happily to herself as she did so. This had always been her favorite time of year, and she already had plenty of ideas for how to decorate the store over the weekend.

To think. At her age, having a new reason to look forward to Christmas. She hadn't expected to feel that way until Melanie made her a grandmother. *That won't be for a long time.* She smiled to herself before checking her phone for any new messages.

"Oh, no!"

Sam hurried in from the living room when he heard her cry of dismay. Tyler heard, too, and came from his room. "What is it?" He looked over her shoulder, where she scrolled through dozens of texts from Melanie.

There's something wrong.

Where are you? Why aren't you answering your phone?

Mom, I'm scared. He's in really bad shape.

"Annie?" Sam touched her shoulder. "What is it?"

She answered without looking up from the phone. "There's something wrong with Edwin."

CHAPTER TEN

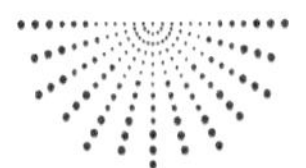

"I swear, if this is all my fault, I don't know what I'll do."

"If you don't stop pacing, you're going to wear a hole in the floor." From the corner of her eye, she caught Sam casting a worried look toward Tyler.

"You should sit down." Tyler's voice was quieter, rich with understanding. "Instead of coffee, maybe I'll fix you some tea."

Tea wasn't going to help. Nothing would until she knew for sure Edwin was alright. The pit in her stomach was more than the result of too much pumpkin pie. "She didn't go into detail." Again, Annie scrolled through the messages. There was no indication of what exactly was wrong with her ex-husband, only that something was. Something very bad, bad enough that Melanie had texted her frantically for the better part of half an hour before suddenly stopping.

For the third or fourth time, Annie tried calling her. "Hey, Mel. I'm sorry, I turned my phone off for dinner. Please, call me soon as you get this. Let me know what's happening."

Though there was no way for Melanie to answer the question screaming loudest at the forefront of her mother's mind.

Did this have something to do with Gavin?

"She'll get back to you as soon as she can." Sam got up, hands thrust in his pockets where Annie could see them curl into fists. "He'll be fine."

"You don't know that. God, what if this is all my fault?"

Sam's brow furrowed, one corner of his mouth pulling up in an expression of confusion. "Why would it be your fault? Why aren't you telling me?"

So many things. He knew nothing about Gavin because she had deliberately avoided telling him. What would it look like if she confessed now? That was out of the question, either way. The idea was to keep the people she cared about safe, and one way of doing that was making sure they didn't know about her connection to a wealthy, powerful, and vindictive man.

Still, Sam waited for an answer.

"It's a long story," she murmured. It was a lame, pitiful response, but it was the best she could do at the moment.

She began pacing again, wringing her hands together, her phone on the coffee table where she'd see it as soon as the screen lit up. Sam cut her off, stepping in front of her—and when she attempted to turn around and pace in the other direction, he held her in place with both hands on her shoulders. "I need you to tell me something. Be honest, please. Are you still in love with him?"

The question surprised her to the point where she blurted out a laugh that brought to mind a braying donkey. She regretted it the moment he winced. "No, I'm sorry. That's the last thing on my mind. I'm not in love with him. I don't even like him."

He didn't look convinced. "So what's with all the hand wringing and blaming yourself?"

"It's a long story."

"I have nowhere else to be."

It was so tempting. Looking up into his earnest,

concerned face, a face she had come to enjoy very much. A face very dear to her. She wanted nothing more than to unburden herself—and she knew he would accept that burden, lessen it for her, offer to help.

Look what had happened to other people she'd involved in her crazy life. Gavin had burned down an entire business, for heaven's sake. He had Norton beaten in prison. He was that powerful, so connected he'd been aware of the young man's existence and of how to get to him. What happened if he decided Sam was a threat, a private investigator digging a little too close? And no matter how she begged Sam to keep his nose out of it, he wouldn't. She knew him too well to believe otherwise.

"No matter what happened, it wasn't your fault." Tyler came in with a cup of tea which he left on the coffee table beside her phone. "You need to stop blaming yourself for someone else's decisions."

Sam grunted like he was frustrated before turning away, going to the door and staring out. There couldn't possibly be anything out there in the dark to hold his interest. She was beginning to regret having him over. It would've meant avoiding this discomfort on top of what was already a stomach-churning situation.

When the phone lit up, Annie scrambled and almost dropped it in her haste. "Mel? Sweetheart?"

"Sorry. I couldn't get a signal in the hospital."

Annie closed her eyes, holding a hand to her forehead. "The hospital. It's that serious? What's wrong?"

"It's okay. He's fine."

Some of the pressure in her chest eased, but not all of it. "What happened, though? Why did you go to the hospital?"

"He thought he was having a heart attack."

"Oh, no." She opened her eyes to look at Tyler, whose eyebrows were nearly up in his hairline. She shook her head slightly and he seemed to understand. "What was it?"

"The doctor said it was just a gallbladder attack. He ate too much, and it made him sick."

Annie snickered. "He always did on Thanksgiving. I should have known. I'm sorry I wasn't here for you, baby."

"It's alright. Everything is okay now." Still, there was a touch of shakiness in Melanie's voice. She must have been terrified until they'd received the diagnosis. And what had happened when she tried to reach out to her mother? She got a voicemail greeting and a bunch of unanswered texts.

Annie promised not to turn her phone off again before thinking to extend well wishes to her ex-husband. "He's too old to be overindulging that way. But don't tell him I said so." Though she secretly hoped Melanie would. How many disapproving looks and soft tongue clicks had Edwin given her over the years? Yet as always, all bets were off when it came to what he wanted. He could eat himself into a gallbladder attack and always come up with an excuse for why he simply had to overindulge.

"It was his gallbladder, but they thought it might be a heart attack." She sank into the couch, leaning her head back with a heavy sigh.

"See? I told you it had nothing to do with you." Sam looked downright exasperated, going so far as to throw his hands into the air. "Would you mind telling me why you thought it did? Did you do something to sabotage him during your trip last weekend?"

"You know I didn't."

"How would I know? That makes about as much sense as you flying off the handle the way you did."

Annie feared things might not end well when she saw Tyler's jaw tighten before he spoke. "You should stop throwing around opinions on things you don't know about."

Sam whirled on him, eyes going narrow. "Maybe I would know about them if somebody would tell me the truth. But it seems like the truth is in short supply lately."

Tyler folded his arms, facing the other man, and dread grew in Annie's belly until she had to speak up. "Okay, okay. Let's retreat to our corners of the ring, boys." It had seemed like things were going so well, too. "Sam has a point. It doesn't make sense for me to fly off the handle the way I did." Then she turned to Sam. "However, I have my reasons. And I would hope by now that you'd understand and respect why I might want to keep things to myself. Don't you know me well enough by now?"

"Don't you know *me*? What do I have to do to earn your trust?"

"That's not what this is about."

"And how would I know that?"

"I think I need to... do anything but be in this room at this moment." Tyler made a quick exit, and that was for the best. She didn't want him and Sam fighting but knew Tyler would come to her defense without her asking for help. He already had.

Sam wore what could only be described as an expectant expression, even tapping his foot on the floor. "Well? I'm waiting."

"Where is this coming from?" Annie's voice was hushed with concern. "This isn't like you."

"It's not? And it isn't like you to be so slippery when asked completely normal, reasonable questions."

"I would appreciate it if you would drop the private investigator act for a little while."

"Act?" He looked downright wounded. "That's an interesting choice of words."

"You know what I meant. Don't get caught up in semantics. I need you to respect my wishes. I have my reasons. And as soon as it seems safe enough, I'll tell you everything."

"I need to ask. Are you involved in anything illegal? Is there something really bad you aren't telling me?"

"No. Nothing illegal. I haven't done anything." She chewed her lip, watching him process this. Did he believe her? "I promise. As soon as I can, I'll tell you everything."

"Does this have to do with your family? What did you really find when you went to Texas?"

She sighed, which seemed to be enough of an answer for him. His face fell in time with his heavy sigh. "Fine. If that's how it's going to be, I won't push for answers." Annie had no time to be relieved, however, since he turned to the rack by the door and pulled his coat from the hook.

"You aren't leaving yet."

"I think it might be better if I do." He went out of his way to avoid her gaze as he put the coat on. "Besides, I should check on the dogs. I'll give you a call tomorrow."

"If that's what you want." She met him at the door and was ready for at least a hug, but he offered nothing more than a tight smile that looked more like a grimace. She watched with a sinking heart as he walked down the driveway, fists in his pockets, his chin tucked close to his chest. He was good and furious—and hurt on top of it.

How much longer would her father loom over her life? Would there ever come a time she'd be free of him?

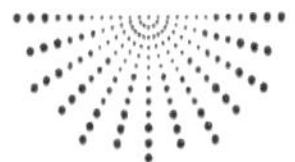

CHAPTER ELEVEN

"I'm telling you. Those Christmas decorations are what's bringing people into the store lately." Rose finished stocking a shelf of brand-new releases before turning toward the elaborate front window. "I work here, and I still can't keep from taking a look at the window when I drive past."

"It's those lights being on the timers that's doing it." Lyle collected empty boxes to be broken down. The store was closed for the day, but they'd stayed later than usual to stock the shelves. Rose was right. They were practically swimming in customers lately.

"I do think it's nice, keeping the twinkle lights running after the store is closed." Annie was rather proud of herself for coming up with the idea. It made no sense for the window to be dark after closing when so many of the shops up and down the street featured glowing windows and lights strung in the trees outside.

With that in mind, she'd outlined the window in white lights, then arranged a handful of slim trees behind it. They featured colorful lights which glowed enticingly throughout the day and night and drew attention to the books displayed in the window.

"They help catch the eye, and when people come back through, they want to step inside to see the decorations up close. It's homey and cheerful." Rose sighed happily as she looked around. "You've created a real homey place here."

"What a shame there's no excuse to keep the decorations up throughout the year." Annie adjusted a few of the tree branches that had been knocked askew by passing customers during the day.

"After this, you can always decorate for Valentine's Day." Lyle waved his hands around. "You know. Hearts and cupids and all that mushy stuff."

"That's true, and we can feature our best-selling romances." Annie's pride swelled. Her employees felt comfortable weighing in and contributing. This store meant more than a paycheck. They wanted to build something lasting.

There was a tree lighting ceremony taking place the following evening, and many of the stores on the block were running sales and specials to entice holiday-minded townsfolk into stopping by. When Annie had brought up the situation with Melanie, her suggestion had involved a hot chocolate bar. "People can come in, get a cup of hot chocolate, maybe browse around a little bit." She even posted about it to the store's social media accounts and linked information on the tree lighting.

"You two go home. I'll finish getting this set up. I get the feeling we'll be pretty busy tomorrow." She waved goodbye to Rose and Lyle through the front window before locking the door. Now that she had the place to herself, she turned up the Christmas music coming through the speakers now hooked up to the playlist on her phone. Tyler had walked her through the setup after Melanie had suggested it, and there was no end to Annie's gratitude. The music and the decorations together never failed to make her smile.

Tonight, she had another reason to smile. She planned to head over to Sam's once everything was in place at the store, and they'd agreed she would spend the night again. Sometimes she felt like a teenager falling in love for the first time. There was still that flutter in her stomach when she looked forward to their time together. She still caught herself checking the clock, counting down the hours until she'd see him.

Only this wasn't like being a teenager, not exactly. Now she had plenty of life experience behind her. It did nothing to lessen her happiness—if anything, she mused as she set up decanters she'd rented for the event, it was a truer kind of happiness. Deeper. She could appreciate him more now that she knew there were very different sorts of men in the world, men who would build a life with a woman while simultaneously chipping away at her, day by day. That wasn't Sam.

Her phone buzzed with an incoming message—for one moment, she wondered if Sam was somehow reading her mind. Did he know she was thinking about him at that very second? That was silly, of course, and her silliness was confirmed when she found a text from Tyler. *Just got in. You coming home tonight?*

Right, because she hadn't confirmed with him. Knowing there was someone at home checking on her safety was nicer than she could put into words. One day, she would find a means of thanking him properly for the comfort he granted. He would more than likely point out how generous it was, allowing him to live with her rent-free.

Though if his business kept growing the way it had been, he might not need her help much longer. In the two weeks since their trip to New Jersey, he'd landed himself five new customers needing help with various jobs around their homes. All it had taken was Mildred's high esteem, then the word of mouth which began to spread as her old friends had taken her word for his good work and strong character. Annie wondered if he would have ever found customers otherwise, between his skittishness when it came to strangers and his rather intimidating appearance. She knew better now than to ever judge him based on his tattoos, of course, but there was no forgetting the first impression she'd had of him back at the museum. It seemed like a dozen years had gone by since then. How far they'd come.

I'll be down the street. He knew what that meant without her needing to explain. *Is that okay?*

He didn't keep her waiting. *And if it wasn't? Of course it's okay. Just making sure.*

As an afterthought, Annie sent him one last message. *Are you coming to the tree lighting tomorrow? Will I see you around?*

He didn't have to think about that, either. *Sure*

thing. I'll come in to see you. She smiled, then left her phone on the counter before returning to the hot chocolate station. She'd stopped at the store that morning and picked up various add-ins: candy canes, marshmallows, and the like. It would probably be better to wait until morning to take them from their packaging, she reasoned, so she left the bags on the table near the back of the store along with the decorated bowls she'd bought to display them.

Setting the station up back there served two purposes: it would lessen the chance of a traffic jam by the front door, and it gave customers a reason to walk past shelves of books on the way to and from. Throughout the day, the three of them had rearranged the rows leading back to the hot chocolate, making it a point to feature what Rose referred to as 'giftable' books. Histories, biographies, plus a shelf entirely devoted to books written by local authors. It had surprised Annie to learn there were so many.

It further surprised her to look at the clock and find it was close to 7:30. She texted Sam, wincing as she did so. *I'm sorry, I lost track of time. Adding extra touches to the decorations. I'll be wrapping up soon.*

Rather than text, he called her. "Sorry, but you

know I'd rather have a conversation than go back and forth that way."

"You know you don't need to apologize. I'm only sorry to keep you waiting this long."

"No need. Good things come to those who wait, right?"

It was corny, but it didn't fail to make her smile. "Should I pick up something on the way? Have you eaten?"

"I was waiting for you and was going to ask you the same question. It doesn't seem fair for you to make another stop on the way when I'm not doing anything. How does Chinese sound?"

"Like heaven. Thank you."

"The usual?"

The fact that he knew her order by heart touched her deeply. A moment ago, she'd considered him corny. It seemed she was developing a corny streak in her later years, as well. "Yes, please. I'm going to lock up soon. I only wanted to place the last of these ornaments on the front display." She nestled another shining ball in a pile of fake snow. The twinkle lights reflected off its surface the way they did off the others until the entire front window practically sparkled.

"It's managed. I'll see you soon." Before ending

the call, he added one final comment. "I've been looking forward to it all week." His voice was close to a growl.

She bit her lip as warmth flooded her cheeks. "So have I." That was another interesting aspect of their relationship, the way his absence during the week made the time they were able to spend together that much more precious.

And exciting. It was most definitely exciting.

Though eventually, spending weekends together wouldn't be enough. She frowned at herself, at the change in the direction her thoughts had taken. Wasn't it enough to enjoy things the way they were? Thinking too far into the future would get her nowhere. The fact was, they enjoyed each other's company. Whatever instant chemistry had sprung up between them was more than enough for the time being. She didn't need anything serious, just as she didn't think Sam did, either. He had certainly been through his fair share of relationship troubles, the way she had.

Knowing Sam would be waiting got her moving faster. She turned off the store lights but left the decorations flickering. They would turn off at midnight, as per the timers she and her employees had so carefully set. A sense of true pride and peace settled over her as she looked around the store, smiling contentedly and looking forward to what was sure to be a busy but fun Sunday.

That was exactly what went through her head a moment before the back door screeched open.

She froze. It wasn't a trick of the wind. There was no mistaking the squealing of the hinges back there. "Hello?" Her voice echoed in the otherwise quiet store. "Who's there?"

At first, there was silence. She went to the front door and closed her hand around the knob, prepared to make a run for it. A glance through the window revealed an empty street, no surprise at this time on a Saturday night. Most of the locals would be at restaurants on the other side of town, where Sam was at this very moment picking up their dinner.

"Help..." The sound was almost too faint to hear, but Annie picked it up. "Can you help me?"

It was a girl's voice, perhaps a child. A number of ugly images raced through Annie's mind, but still, she crept toward the back of the store instead of running. She'd already been through enough ugly surprises to temper her natural curiosity.

"Do you need an ambulance? I'll call one for you." From where she stood, Annie could make out a huddled figure wedged between the door frame and the door itself. Her slight build told Annie this was a young woman. She wore a thick coat and a knit cap which either covered a bald head or hid her hair. She shivered violently, rocking back and forth while moaning softly.

"Please. I crashed my car. My car is ruined. I hit my head, I think."

She sounded young enough that she could be Melanie's age. That was what got Annie moving, the thought of her daughter being in a situation like this and needing help. She trotted back to the door, then got down on one knee beside the girl.

And that was her mistake.

She didn't see the brick in the girl's hand until it was too late, until it was already on its way to crashing against the side of her head.

CHAPTER TWELVE

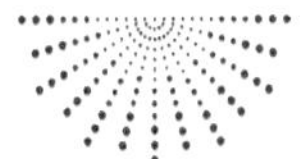

"I really am sorry, but this is the only way to make him understand."

Annie heard the voice but didn't recognize it. Her head was so heavy, her eyelids seemingly glued shut. No matter how she tried, there was no opening them.

And when she attempted to raise her head, she regretted it. Fireworks went off, a gong rang out, and she was nearly overcome by a wave of fierce nausea.

"No, just rest. Go to sleep. It will all be over soon."

What would be over soon? Annie struggled to ask the question along with so many others, but it was like trying to swim upstream through a deadly current. The harder she struggled, the more ground she lost. Maybe the girl was right. Maybe it would be better to give in and let sleep claim her.

It was only a nagging voice at the back of her head it kept her from doing so. There was danger, she was in danger, she couldn't forget it. There were footsteps all around her, and somewhere, somebody was burning something. A fire pit, maybe, or a barbecue grill. But no, it wasn't the right time of year for that, not even down here where temperatures didn't get as cold as they did back home. But this was her home now, right? Not New Jersey, not anymore.

Again, she began to drift off. It was easier than trying to make sense of her confused thoughts. All she needed was to sleep. She would feel better once she woke up.

You won't wake up.

That thought—crystal clear and as glaring as a stop sign—snapped her eyelids open. What was she doing? Lying here on the floor at the back of the store. She blinked rapidly, willing her vision to come back into focus, but her will was not enough.

No, it wasn't her eyesight that was at fault, was it? It was smoke getting in the way.

"I really am sorry."

Annie turned her head in the direction of the voice, and the girl gave a start.

"You're not supposed to be awake."

"Alex?" It was the first time she'd really seen the girl's face, and even now there was too much smoke to make her out clearly, but Annie would have bet her life on it. "Why?"

The girl didn't say a word, choosing instead to slip out through the back door without another glance. Leaving Annie in what she now understood was meant to be her tomb.

She tried to get to her feet but only fell to her knees again. She was too dizzy, the world spinning around her. Getting out was the most important thing, and she knew it, but she knew something else as well. She had worked too hard and put too much of her heart into this store to let it burn to the ground.

That was why instead of opening the back door and crawling into the alley, she crawled beneath the smoke. An entire shelf of books burned bright, the flames licking the set of shelves beside it. Annie let out a grief-filled wail that quickly became a series of hacking coughs. The fire extinguisher was behind the counter. She flailed around until finally, her left shoulder bumped against it. She felt around with her hands, getting her bearings, before crawling behind the counter and finding the extinguisher in its customary location.

The smoke was too thick and thicker all the time. She could barely breathe, much less concentrate on working the extinguisher. It was too late, but no, it couldn't be too late! Not when she had worked so hard!

There had to be something she could do, but first, she had to breathe. She got low on the floor, gulping in as much clean air as she could, but even that was a losing battle. The smoke, lack of oxygen, and the wound on her head all combined to disorient her. She touched the side of her face to the floor, wracked with painful coughs, and all she could think about was Melanie. What would Melanie do when she heard?

"Annie!"

That couldn't be real. She was imagining it, someone calling her name. Another painful bout of coughing left her too weak to move, much less to call out.

"Annie! Where are you? Tell me where you are!"

Sam. It was Sam. She knew it, she felt it, and his presence gave her the strength it took to keep crawling from behind the counter. She tried to call his name. All that came out was more coughing and gasping.

But it was enough. A moment later, she was in his arms, and he was picking her up and carrying her from the store. Flashing red lights painted the walls, the sidewalk, the trees. Firefighters rushed past, shouting instructions, while a crowd began to gather on the other side of the street.

"Annie." Sam sat her on the curb, allowing her to lean against him when the act of sitting up was too much. A pair of hands placed a mask over her nose and mouth. Oxygen. She gulped it gratefully, though every breath meant more coughing. Her skin and clothes were streaked with soot and her head felt as though it were about to split in two.

But she was alive. And the thought of how close she'd come to losing her life made her dissolve in tears against Sam's shoulder.

~

"The damage looks a lot worse than it is." Kevin slid his phone into his pocket upon rejoining Annie and Sam in her curtained-off section of the emergency room. "There is very little structural damage due to the fire, but the water was another story."

He slid Annie a pained look, the sort of person wore when they didn't want to add insult to injury. "It looks like you'll be out of business for a little while."

"A little while? And we're supposed to be getting ready for Christmas." A fresh bout of coughing resulted from her outburst. It felt as if someone was jumping on her ribs.

Sam adjusted her oxygen mask, scowling. "There's a reason they want you to wear this. And to not upset yourself."

"How am I supposed to react?"

"I'm sorry to be the bearer of bad news." Kevin did look sorry. "It shouldn't be long, though."

"Was it the lights?" Sam jammed his hands into his pockets, his eyes darting over Kevin's face like a man desperate for answers. "A malfunction, maybe?"

"It wasn't a malfunction." Annie lowered the mask again. This was the first time they'd been alone, not to mention the fact that until now she hadn't been able to say more than a word or two at a time before choking on smoke.

"You know what happened?" Both men looked to her, brows lifted expectantly.

"It was her." She looked to Sam. "The girl."

He went pale. "Alex?"

Kevin held up a hand. "Who is Alex?"

"A girl who has a grudge against Sam." She closed her eyes and concentrated as hard as she could, searching her memory. "She said something about this being the only way to make you understand."

"Make me understand what?"

"I'm sorry, but I didn't get the chance to ask. It might have had something to do with trying to stay alive." Sam recoiled slightly, and she regretted her harsh words. "I'm sorry. I don't mean to take it out on you. But that's all she said."

"Maybe we'd better start from the beginning." Kevin drew up one of two molded plastic chairs and took a seat before pulling his phone out once again. He tapped the screen a few times before placing the phone on the bed, face up. He'd opened a voice memo app.

"I don't remember much."

"I need you to tell me everything you can remember." He tapped the red button, beginning the recording. It took some time thanks to the amount of coughing she did, but slowly she told the story. Finding the girl at the back door, wanting to help her. The brick.

"We found a brick in the alley behind the store." Kevin shared a grim look with Sam. "There was blood on it."

"That would explain this." Annie touched gentle fingers to a fresh set of stitches on her scalp. "Much more of this and I'll look like Frankenstein." What was intended to be a laugh sounded more like a choked sob.

Sam reached over and squeezed her hand.

It gave her the strength to continue. "The next thing I knew, I regained consciousness and already there was smoke in the store. She was still there. That was when she told me this was the only way to make Sam understand. But she didn't elaborate." Stringing that many sentences together exhausted her. She sank back against the pillows, out of breath.

"And she left you there?"

"Yes, she did. She told me to go back to sleep."

Sam turned away, muttering profanity strong enough to make her blush. She had never heard him talk that way before. "This isn't your fault." He flinched but said nothing, keeping his back to her.

"Why didn't you leave the store immediately?"

She turned back to Kevin. "I wanted to try to put the fire out if I could. I was too dizzy to stand, anyway. I crawled across the store and found the extinguisher, but by then the smoke was too thick."

She raised her voice slightly and spoke directly to the back of Sam's head. "If it hadn't been for Sam coming in, I would have died. He saved my life." Aside from the rising and falling of his shoulders as he breathed, he didn't move.

"And it's a good thing he got there when he did. Can you describe the girl for me?" Annie laid out a description, right down to the forest green cap Alex wore to cover her hair.

Sam let out a grunt, turning part way to look at Kevin. "I can do better than that. I can tell you where she lives. I'd like to go with you and have a few words."

"With all due respect, we won't be doing that. That might be the worst course of action." Color rose in Sam's face, but Kevin only shook his head. "Let us handle it. All you need is for her to accuse you of coming around and threatening her to make this whole situation more complicated than it already is."

"He's right." Annie nudged Sam with her foot, the closest thing to where he stood. "That will only make things worse. Let them do their jobs."

"You mean the way you let the firefighters do their jobs while you escaped safely?"

"That isn't the same. I was trying to save my store."

"And I was trying to save... forget it." He folded his arms, and Annie noticed the way he positioned himself far enough from her bed that she couldn't reach him anymore.

Kevin blew out a long sigh, standing and pocketing his phone. "We'll find her. Don't worry. She won't come anywhere near you again."

"Thank you."

He cast a doleful look her way, lowering his brow. "Just make me a promise, would you? Don't try to handle this on your own, for once."

"I'll do my best." It was enough to make him snicker, which was what she'd intended.

The store would have to close. Just when things were going so well. And she'd been so looking forward to the tree lighting and the customers and even the stupid hot chocolate station. It had been a good idea, hadn't it? Maybe next year—if she still had a store by next year.

That was not what she needed to ponder at that exact moment, but there was no shaking the fear off now. She had lost stock. She would need to have repairs done, certainly. How would she afford any of it? Arson wasn't covered by insurance. What would she do?

Rather than voice that question, she decided to indulge her curiosity regarding a topic Sam could help with. "How did you know to come for me? You were supposed to be picking up dinner."

It was enough to shake Sam from his closed-off state. He slapped a palm to his forehead. "I forgot. I'll have to call and add it to the report."

"Add what to the report?"

"I got a phone call. A man told me to go to the store, that you would need help. He told me to hurry. I never did pick up the food. I didn't even make it to the restaurant."

Annie fairly tingled as the truth behind Sam's explanation sank in. It couldn't be, but who else would do that? Who would know what Alex had planned? Was Gavin watching?

If so, he didn't even have the guts to save his daughter himself. He had to call in reinforcements.

"Did you recognize the voice?" She knew the answer would be no, but she asked anyway. Just in case.

"I never heard it before, and it came up as an unknown number." He went through his phone, then nodded and held it out. The call had come in at around a quarter to eight, not long after she had Sam had spoken. Somewhere around the time she was unconscious, perhaps, while Alex started the fire.

He shrugged. "I figured it could be a quack, but I didn't want to take the chance. I'm glad I didn't."

"Me, too."

"I guess she must be working with somebody. A boyfriend, maybe. Somebody who got cold feet at the last minute."

Yes, he could believe that if he wanted to. It might even be the truth, for all she knew, but she suspected it wasn't. If her father wasn't in town, he would have somebody watching for him. He always had.

For now, it would be better for Sam if he believed the safer option. The one which wouldn't end with him tangling with Gavin. "Thank goodness for cold feet, I guess."

"When I think what might have happened if I hadn't taken it seriously." Though he tipped his head to the side, frowning in confusion. "Then again, I guess he called the fire department, too. Or else why would they have gotten there at the same time I did?"

"I suppose he must have made the call." How had

Gavin found Sam? How did he know his phone number? So many questions. Would she ever get answers?

Sam took the chair Kevin had vacated, unaware of the questions plaguing her. "No matter what happens, we'll find a way for you to bounce back. I have no doubt Miss Rose will start a donation drive for you. It wouldn't surprise me one bit if she went around the lighting ceremony asking for money."

"Do you honestly think she would do that?" The idea made Annie smile. It was almost too easy to imagine the gentle but assertive woman cajoling townspeople into donating whatever cash they had on hand.

He leaned in, running a hand over the top of her head. "If she hasn't already thought about it, I'll give her the idea." He lifted the mask from Annie's face and planted a soft but lingering kiss against her lips.

It wasn't quite what she'd had in mind for the evening, but considering how things could have turned out, it wasn't half bad.

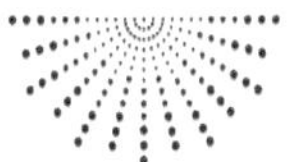

CHAPTER THIRTEEN

Rose and Lyle did better than pass an old coffee can around during the tree lighting ceremony, as Annie had imagined.

"The donations are up to over three thousand bucks!" Tyler shook his head, wearing a smile wide enough to light up his face. "It's like a miracle, huh?"

He held out his phone as proof. Annie could hardly believe the total on the donation site where Lyle had created a fundraiser. *Help Us Rebuild Our Bookstore*. Not the catchiest title, but it got the point across.

"Is that going to be enough, do you think?" Tyler looked and sounded touchingly hopeful.

"I wish I could say for sure, but it will certainly help."

"Don't forget, they collected almost five hundred dollars at the tree lighting ceremony, too." Tyler settled in at the other end of the sofa.

Annie tried not to roll her eyes at the way Bogart immediately hopped into place, curling up beside him.

"You ungrateful thing." She scowled at the cat, who could not have cared less for her opinion. That was nothing new.

"What can I say? He knows who he likes." Tyler petted his head, earning himself a lick on the hand.

"We'll see what happens the next time you come sniffing around for food." In response, Bogart merely stretched languidly before engaging in a bath, starting with the paws. "I don't know why I love you."

"How is your head?" Tyler's question had tripped from his tongue more times in the past week than Annie could count. She appreciated his concern and didn't want to think about a life in which there was no one around to care how she was feeling, but the sense of constantly being watched and fretted over was beginning to fray her nerves.

"Much better. Really, you don't have to worry about me." She held up her phone, wearing a weary smile. "Just like I told Melanie after her last text. I'm starting to think she has an hourly timer set on her phone, prompting her to reach out."

"It can't be easy on her, knowing you had yet another close call."

"I know, I know. And it makes me feel terrible, knowing I've caused the people who care about me so much concern. It isn't like I go out of my way to get in these situations."

"You should FaceTime her tonight while we're putting the tree together. That might help her feel better, seeing you decorating and getting into the holiday."

"That's not a bad idea. I don't know what I would do without you." He ducked his head, obviously pleased but shy when it came to expressing that pleasure. Rather than reply, he picked up his phone again. From where she sat, Annie could see the fundraising website a moment before Tyler refreshed the page.

And when he did, the results sent him sitting bolt upright. Bogart jumped up, startled, and darted across the room.

"What's wrong?" For one sick moment, Annie imagined finding out the fundraiser was shut down. That they might have violated the rules of the site, something like that. Was it possible for people to change their minds and take their money back?

He looked up from the phone, his face slack, mouth hanging open. When words failed him, he thrust the phone at her. The number on the screen made her eyes bulge.

"It has to be a fluke. A bug or something." Because certainly, there was no way three thousand dollars had suddenly changed to twenty-three thousand.

"There was a donation. A big one." He leaned over, pointing to the list of contributors. Sure enough, an anonymous donor had pledged twenty-thousand dollars only a few minutes ago.

"I should've known." Annie put the phone down before she could drop it, her hands shaking. Now that the shock had worn off, the truth was obvious. "I can't believe it took this long for him to stick his nose back into my life, honestly."

"But this is a good thing. Right?"

"Is it?" She closed her eyes, the rise in blood pressure making her head ache. While she had improved greatly since the night of the attack, the headaches still came and went.

"You know you need the money. Rose and Lyle

need to get paid. So do you. And you'll need it to help restock and replace any damaged equipment."

"But we both know where the money came from." She lifted one eyelid, looking his way. "I mean, he's the only one who could do it."

"Of course. I figured it went without saying."

"You mean you think it's a good idea for me to take money from him?"

"Honestly? I think it's a good idea to put your pride aside and do what needs to be done."

"Do you honestly think that's all this is about? My pride? Tyler, this man has hurt people out of some twisted sense of fatherly duty. He's followed me my entire life."

He sighed. "I know."

"If I accept this money, it's the same as accepting everything he's done. I can't condone him having Norton beaten, no matter what Norton did to me. It wasn't his place. It wasn't his place to burn down that bar we visited in Texas, or to attack a stupid kid who tried to force himself on me years ago. I don't even know how many examples there are, times he influenced my life without my even knowing about it. I take his money, and it's all okay. I can't do that."

"I'm no expert, but it seems to me you can't pick

and choose which donations you accept and which you don't."

"I know."

"What do you want to do? Shut down the entire fundraiser?"

She groaned, her misery depinning. "No. We can't do that."

"You don't know for sure it was Gavin."

It took counting to five in her head to keep from snapping. "Let's not kid each other. We both know it was him. Who else would have that much money to donate all at once? I certainly don't know of anyone who would."

"That makes one of us, since I have so many rich friends."

She blurted out a laugh, relieved when Tyler joined her. "I want to do the right thing. That's all."

"I know you do." He reached over and rubbed her arm briefly, briskly. "You always do, I reckon."

"And accepting this money could be considered the same as accepting his interference. I don't want to give him that idea. I don't want him in my life."

"You could try reaching out to him."

"How would I do that? I don't have an address or phone number."

He winced. "Is it wrong that the first thing to

come to mind was putting a great, big sign in your front window? Since, you know, he probably has somebody checking on the house for him?"

She shook her head. "A little wrong, yes."

"But not an entirely bad idea."

The ringing of the doorbell startled them both. "If this is some thick-necked goon from Texas…" Tyler motioned for her to remain on the sofa while he went to the door. Brief murmuring led to his stepping back to allow Sam's entrance.

"Hi. I didn't expect you for hours." His arrival meant the end of Gavin talk, which Annie supposed was a good thing.

They weren't getting anywhere, and the more she thought about the money, the more trapped she'd feel. The man seemed determined to control her life —yet he would never stoop so low as to reach out over the phone and ask how his daughter managed to sleep at night when the memory of choking on smoke was so fresh.

Rather than kiss her hello or even offer a hug, Sam ran both hands through his hair. There was a sickly pallor to his sweat-slick face. "Something happened."

It was sheer muscle memory, the way she jumped up from the sofa. Too many years as a mother, watching Melanie make the face Sam was. "You're going to be sick, aren't you? Come with me." She took him by the arm and began pulling him toward the kitchen since the sink was closer than the bathroom.

He planted his feet. "No, I'm fine. Just shaken up."

"What's wrong?"

"I don't know how to say this, because I'm not sure what it means or if it means anything at all. The timing is so strange. I had to come straight here and tell you."

"Spit it out." Tyler wasn't known for his patience, though Annie was on the verge of saying the same thing.

"I've spent this week looking for Alex." He offered Annie an apologetic shrug which she quickly waved off.

"I thought you might be. Did you find her?"

"I found her, alright." He drew a deep breath. "She was run off the road last Sunday morning. I found her in the ICU."

"Run off the road?" Annie shivered, though she didn't know why. Should she feel any sympathy for a girl who'd tried to kill her?

"That was what she said when she regained consciousness, which wasn't for a day and a half after her car was discovered. There was damage to the rear bumper that corroborated her story."

Annie glanced at Tyler, whose stormy expression told her all she needed to know about his interpretation of events. "It couldn't have happened to a nicer person." He returned Annie's stare, his eyes narrowing. "I can't say I'm sorry."

"That's an interesting choice of words."

Tyler's head snapped back before he turned to Sam. "What does that mean?"

"Where were you last Sunday morning?"

"Wait a minute." Annie laughed in disbelief. "You don't think he had something to do with it."

"Of course he does." Tyler shook his head as he looked the other man up and down. His lips pulled back in a knowing smirk. "He assumes I have it in me to do something like that. Some people get an idea in their head, and there's no convincing them otherwise."

"Did it occur to you I'm asking because I would have loved to do the same thing myself? You think I didn't go straight to Alex's last known address the minute Annie was settled in here at home?"

Tyler took a step toward him. "Then maybe I should ask you where you were last Sunday morning."

Sam copied Tyler, stepping closer. Now they were nearly toe-to-toe. "I drove all the way back here. And you weren't here when I arrived, if you remember."

Tyler leaned in until their noses were nearly touching. "I went to the store for groceries. You were here when I came back with them."

Annie held her hands to her head. "Would you both stop? For heaven's sake. Stand down. This is all ridiculous." She tapped Sam's shoulder. "Exactly how would he have run Alex off the road, then come home with no damage to my car?"

"Thank you." Tyler lifted his chin, sneering at Sam.

"This is all my fault." Suddenly, she felt very tired. Very old, and very tired. "This is all too much."

"There you go again, taking the blame for something that has nothing to do with you." Sam rubbed a hand through his hair, grunting. "Why do you keep doing that?"

There was nothing left to be done. She had to tell him. She'd already waited too long, it seemed. Now he was blaming Tyler for Gavin's wrongdoing. "It must have been my father. It had to be."

Sam blurted out a laugh. "Your father? Is that what you think this is about?"

"Very much so. This is what I didn't want to tell you about before."

The disbelief melted away from his face, quickly replaced by suspicion. "You think your father is capable of something like this?"

"My father is capable of a lot of things." It was the middle of the day, and she more than likely should have stayed away from alcohol, but suddenly a glass of wine was in order. She went straight to the kitchen without asking either of the men if they wanted a drink. By the time they joined her, she was already uncorking a bottle of merlot.

"Maybe you should take it easy with that." Annie ignored Sam's advice, pouring herself a healthy glass.

"Forgive me if I'm not in the mood to hear what I should or shouldn't do just now." She took a sip, followed by a deep breath. "I need you to understand I kept this from you because I knew you would look for him, and that's the last thing you should do. My father isn't who I thought he was all these years. The man I believed was my father is really my uncle, Tyler's father." Another sip to bolster her. "And he's much worse than Cal. He's been following me all my life, interfering. I believe it was one of his men who called and told you to help me, and for all I know it was the same man who ran Alex off the road at my father's instruction."

Poor Sam. Her heart went out to him as he tried to make sense of this. He looked to Tyler for confirmation, and his face crumpled in further confusion when Tyler only nodded. "Maybe I could use a drink, come to think of it."

By the time Annie finished telling her story, including the handful of examples of Gavin's interference over the years, the three of them were seated around the living room. She finished off by showing Sam the anonymous donation they'd received earlier in the day. "A man that wealthy? It would be a drop in the bucket to him. I have no doubt he was behind this, as well."

He'd been quiet ever since she'd poured him the wine. She imagined it was his experience as an investigator that made him such a keen listener. Never once had he interrupted, allowing her and Tyler to tell the full story uninterrupted.

It was his silence once the story was complete that set her heart pounding. "Please try to understand. I didn't want him hurting you in any way, and if you came too close to him, he might have done that. I don't know a way to get in touch with him and tell him to stop, so I couldn't protect you."

Tyler grunted in agreement. "The guy is bad news, and he has a lot of resources at his disposal."

"Please. I didn't want to lie to you." She watched him intently, her heart in her throat, her palms sweating. What if he decided to leave and never come back?

He stared at the floor, his jaw twitching. She opened her mouth, ready to beg him to say something, anything, but Tyler caught her eye and shook his head. Maybe he was right. Maybe Sam needed time to think.

It didn't take much time. "What are we going to do about this?"

His use of the word *we* nearly brought her to tears. Rather than thank him as she wanted to, she addressed his question. "I'm not sure. Like I said, I don't have any way to call or email him. I'm sure I could find out where he lives, but I doubt it's the sort of setup where I could march up to the front door and be allowed inside. He's gone out of his way my entire life to avoid seeing me."

Tyler snickered. "Coward. He'd rather follow you around and terrorize everybody else in your life."

"So that's why you thought Edwin was your fault." Sam leaned forward, elbows on his knees, and laced his fingers behind his neck. "Now I get it."

"I really did want to tell you. But don't pretend you wouldn't have searched for him."

"Fine. I won't pretend." At last, he turned to her and looked her in the eye. "I want to find him. I want to bring this to an end for you. He needs to know how you feel about him interfering in your life."

"It's too dangerous. Look how far he's willing to go!"

"How far would he go if you were with me at the time?"

"Do you think that's a good idea?" Tyler looked stricken, perhaps remembering what he'd already witnessed. How far Gavin would go.

Still, there was no avoiding what needed to be done. Now that Sam had mentioned it, it seemed the most logical option. Gavin would never accept instructions from a third party.

But from his daughter?

She offered Tyler a weak shrug. "I think it's the only option I have."

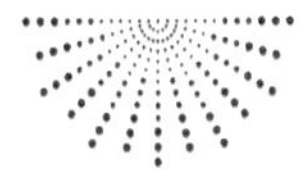

CHAPTER FOURTEEN

"This sounds like a terrible idea."

It was a good thing Annie had swallowed her tea before Mildred gave her opinion. "You narrowly avoided a face full of orange pekoe."

"How is that?"

"Never mind."

"Whatever gave you the notion to purchase tickets for whatever gala Gavin is throwing?" Annie noted the slight tremble of Mildred's teacup when she set it down on the table between them. The older woman might have been advanced in years, but tremors were something new. Annie suspected they were situational.

"It's the only sure way of getting in front of him. Somewhere there's a lot of people. Society people like him. He would never expect me there, and if he tries to throw me out, his cronies will find out more about him than he wants them to know."

"It's too risky."

"I'll have Sam there with me."

"It's too risky for both of you. For heaven's sake, you know what he's capable of. Do you think that's where it stops?" Mildred's chin began to tremble the way her hands did.

Annie reached for her hands, rubbing the backs of her fingers with both thumbs. "Please, don't be upset. He's not going to hurt me. I'm the last person he wants to hurt. What he wants is to avoid me. I'm going to make sure he can't. That's all."

"And Sam?"

"Of course, he refuses to let me go by myself. And when I reminded him of what Gavin has done in the past, he flipped it around and reminded me he's already on Gavin's radar. He had his phone number and everything, and I'm sure his research didn't end there."

"So he's already at risk."

It twisted Annie up inside to hear that, though she knew it was true. Simply by being part of her life, Sam was in danger. "Sam has never hurt me.

That's always been a prerequisite for Gavin harming somebody close to me."

"You have that much faith that he'll stick with precedent on this?"

While inside, Annie withered under her friend's scrutiny, she kept a straight spine. "I have to. Otherwise, I'll chicken out and never face him."

"Is it really so bad, though? Knowing he's watching over you?"

"Yes. It is."

"Even though you know he's only trying to help you?"

"Are you that worried?"

Mildred lifted a thin shoulder, looking frightened and vulnerable. "I would rather not lose you, if you wouldn't mind."

"You aren't going to lose me. I'm not going anywhere. But I simply can't allow him to interfere anymore. You have to understand that."

Mildred averted her eyes, her lips in a tight line which Annie took to mean she understood—but still didn't agree. "Now I remember how it feels to be Melanie's age."

Mildred quirked an eyebrow. "What does that mean?"

"I remember what it was like having to go ahead

with something I wanted to do, but Mom disapproved of." Annie chuckled softly as she reached for her tea. "It was about as frustrating as this is now."

"I suppose it wouldn't be enough to make you change your mind."

"I only want to see him. That's all. Just to have a few words. And then we're going to come right back and I'll finish getting ready for Christmas." The thought still pained her. She couldn't help but remember all the plans she'd made for the Christmas season. At least they had the money from the fundraiser, so she could pay her employees rather than leave them high and dry at maybe the worst time of year.

But she hadn't yet touched the money from her anonymous donor. She wanted it available in case there was any way to return it to Gavin. When she told him she wouldn't use it, she at least wanted to be telling the truth that she hadn't touched it yet.

"So you expect to stroll into a charity ball unnoticed?"

"I'm sure there will be tight security, but it isn't as if the event is being held at Gavin's house. They'll use whatever security system is on hand at the location."

"You sound like Sam."

"That's not surprising, since most of this is his doing. He has a friend who lives out there, and they purchased the tickets so neither of our names will even be on the guest list."

Mildred tilted her head to the side, nodding. "Shrewd, I'll give him that."

"He knows what he's doing. I have faith in him."

"And when is your flight?"

"We fly in first thing in the morning."

Additional concern furrowed Mildred's brow. "Are you sure you're up to that?"

"It's been almost two weeks since the attack. I'm just fine." She turned her head to the side, gesturing to the place where her stitches used to be. "My hair even covers up the spot they shaved off."

Mildred didn't look impressed. Perhaps this was the way it would have to be. Fighting to make her understand would only lead to hurt feelings and tension. "I found a nice dress. It's very pretty. And hey, when will I ever have the chance to hobnob with society folks?"

She dropped her voice to a whisper. "What do you think they'll say if they know they're rubbing elbows with somebody who used to live in... New Jersey?"

That got Mildred laughing, finally. "Heaven

forbid." Yet instead of dying off, her laughter grew louder.

When she snorted, Annie burst out laughing, too. "It wasn't that funny!"

"It isn't so much what you said." Mildred wiped a tear from her eye, still chuckling. "It's the way you said it—and who it reminded me of. You sounded exactly like Hattie just now."

"I did?"

"She would make a similar joke, no doubt. Trying to make me laugh so I wouldn't be mad at her anymore. She was always acting stubborn and making me want to strangle her." She smiled softly. "And making me laugh until I forgot what I was ticked about."

It seemed her present concerns weren't so easily forgotten, though. She touched her hand to the side of her head, the place where Annie had needed stitches. "What about her?"

"According to Sam's friends in the police department, they'll take her into custody as soon as she's released from the hospital. That should be any day now. She was badly banged up in the crash."

"But they know what she did to you?"

"Her car's GPS has the address to the bookstore in it. And according to phone records, her cell pinged on the very block the store sits on at the time of the fire. It doesn't get much more obvious than that."

"At least you won't have to worry about her anymore."

"I hope that's the end of all of this. The worrying, the near misses, the close calls." Annie debated with herself before deciding to take her fourth cookie. Life was too short to debate with herself over calories. "I would like to not be proven wrong the next time I tell Melanie not to worry about me."

"I've never been one to get preachy, so to speak, but I believe you have business here in this world that you haven't yet finished. You're needed here."

"I hope that doesn't change anytime soon."

"It won't so long as I'm alive and kicking, and I don't plan on going anywhere."

"It will be fine. And I'll finally be able to say I've set eyes on my father. Talk about a Christmas miracle." Annie chuckled at her lame joke, hoping Mildred would join in. She was disappointed.

"Just do me one favor."

"Anything."

Mildred met her gaze, unblinking. "Don't underestimate him."

CHAPTER FIFTEEN

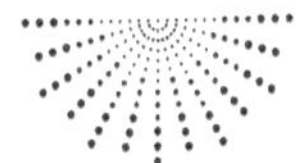

I t wasn't until they stepped out of the Uber in front of the museum that Annie's blood turned cold. She stared up at the imposing structure with its marble columns and lavish Christmas decorations and wondered what in the world she was doing there.

"Are you alright?" Sam joined her, standing close and taking her by the arm.

"It's funny. I was fine all throughout the flight. Did I seem even the least bit nervous at the hotel?"

"You seemed almost alarmingly calm. I told myself you were doing whatever it took to get through this."

"I couldn't wait for tonight to come. I wanted to get it over with more than anything."

"And now?"

"Now I can't move." That wasn't the worst of it. She could hardly breathe. "You might have to carry me."

Instead of doing so, he stepped in front of her. It was the right move, as he filled her field of vision, blocking the museum and the thought of what was behind the massive, iron doors. "We don't have to go in."

"Then we'll have come all this way for nothing."

"I wouldn't say it was for nothing. This is our first trip together. They say your first trip in a new relationship should be a short one in case you find out the two of you are incompatible as travelers." He shrugged, offering a lopsided grin before cupping her shoulders. "Now, we have that taken care of. And I can say I've been to Texas."

"And you'll have wasted all the money on tickets for the event."

"It doesn't mean anything." He lowered his brow, leaning in until their foreheads touched. "I mean it. We can leave right now, order obscene amounts of dessert from room service, and fly back tomorrow."

It was almost too tempting an idea. Mildred would certainly be happy. Tyler might, too—he wasn't so much supportive of their plan as he was accepting of it. Unlike Mildred, he understood there was no amount of arguing that would change Annie's mind. That didn't mean he had to like it.

Her resolve began to slip away with every passing second Sam spent staring into her eyes. "You've been so supportive. I'm sorry I didn't tell you sooner about all of this."

"I've told you before, I understand. You don't have to apologize."

"But we did come all this way."

"We did."

"And I did go through all the trouble of trying to look nice."

"And you do." He pulled his head back to look her up and down, eyes twinkling. She'd decided on a simple red dress with a full skirt that made her feel elegant and sophisticated. It gave her extra confidence, and she would need every ounce. She'd even broken out her mother's pearls, which she hadn't worn since her wedding day. With her hair pulled up and more makeup than she'd had occasion to wear in far too long, she almost felt like a different person.

"You look very nice, yourself." Like the other men now passing by on their way up the grand staircase leading to the entrance, Sam wore a tuxedo. They could have been any well-heeled couple looking the way they did. Instead, they were little better than spies.

Was it wrong that the idea gave her a slight thrill?

"We could go anywhere else and paint the town red if that's what you want to do. This is up to you."

Again, she wrestled with the notion of leaving, but again the thought left her feeling uncomfortable. Unfulfilled. She would only be letting herself down if she turned back now. And it might be her only chance at cornering Gavin somewhere he couldn't get away.

"No." She lifted her chin and threw back her shoulders. "We're going in. I deserve the opportunity to make him hear me."

"You have no idea what it does to me to hear you say things like that." He stepped aside before extending a crooked elbow. "Let's do it, then." She took hold of him, grateful for his strength and stability. She would need it.

Two enormous Christmas trees flanked the museum entrance, but they were outshone by the massive and elaborate tree set up beneath a grand dome in the museum's cavernous lobby. There was an open bar set up on both sides of the room while catering staff carried trays of champagne flutes and appetizers.

Annie did her best to look casual as she studied the room while Sam presented their tickets at the security checkpoint. Where would she find her father? Would he find her first? There was no reason for him to look for her here. He couldn't possibly predict her appearance.

Once they were inside, they stayed close to the walls, moving around the perimeter of the growing crowd. There was a room off to the side of the lobby where items were set up for a silent auction benefiting the children's charity Gavin had chosen to bless with his attention.

"The vain so-and-so." Annie inclined her head toward the giant banner set up just inside the auction room, featuring a smiling Gavin surrounded by—Annie guessed—children who'd already benefited from the charity's efforts.

It was unnerving, looking at him and seeing so much of herself. There was no question as to whether he and Cal were brothers. They shared more than enough in the looks department. But while Cal's features were hard and sharp, Gavin's were softer. His eyes rounder, his nose not so narrow.

"You have his smile." Sam handed her one of two champagne flutes that he'd accepted from a server.

"I can't say that brings me much pleasure." It took all of her resolve not to bolt back the entire glass all at once. She needed to keep her wits about her.

"You have to relax."

"Oh? Whatever makes you say that?" She tried to smile but failed.

"You look like you're here to rob the place, the way you keep looking around all shifty-eyed." He squeezed her hand. "Relax. Breathe. Enjoy the champagne. I know I'll never enjoy champagne this expensive again."

He had a point there. And the sight of so many tempting appetizers reminded her she hadn't eaten since breakfast, too busy having her hair and nails done to remember food. She managed to snag a couple of stuffed mushrooms and a few fried shrimp. "I can't drink on an empty stomach, after all." Sam chuckled but was wise enough not to comment.

According to the website, the doors to the main ballroom would open at 8:00. By five minutes to eight, she was ready to jump out of her skin. Where was he? "You don't think he's seen us on the security feed and decided not to come out, do you?"

"I doubt it. More likely, some security guard would approach us and discreetly ask us to step aside and have a word." He was right, and that hadn't happened yet. By 8:00, when the ballroom doors opened, they were still moving freely through the crowd, slowly but surely creeping out of the lobby.

It took a second for Annie to shake off her shock once they entered the ballroom. "It's like Santa's village in here." Lit trees lined all four walls, with more lights draped across the length of the ceiling. The tables featured tall centerpieces of silver branches hung with crystal snowflakes.

Sam blew out a low whistle. "This is impressive. He doesn't skimp on the expenses." They found their name cards, or rather the name cards belonging to Sam's friend and his wife, before taking another tour of the perimeter. There was an ornate chair set up in front of a silver backdrop, with wrapped boxes stacked on both sides. Pictures with Santa? It was as good a guess as any, though as far as Annie knew there would be no children at this party.

The sound of jingling bells caught her attention before it caught Sam's. She craned her neck, looking around to see where the sound came from. It was only when a spotlight landed on a door at the far corner of the room that Sam pointed. "Here comes Santa Claus." Yes, and the sound of laughter and cheering began to rise up as the man himself made his way through the crowd.

There was no reason for her to know. He wore a red velvet suit, black patent leather boots, a fake beard and all. But she knew who was underneath them.

And she gripped Sam's arm when the realization took hold. "That's him."

"What?" He looked at her, then back at Santa. "That's him? How do you know?"

"I don't know him well, but this is exactly what he would do. Mister Charity, Mister Wonderful." She shook her head slowly, smiling like everyone around them but out of cynicism.

"Yes, now that you put it that way, I wouldn't be surprised. Plus it would explain why he hasn't shown himself before now."

"Exactly. I wonder what he'd do if I strolled over and sat on his lap for a photo."

Sam laughed heartily at this, loud enough that she joined in. "That would be worth capturing for posterity."

To think. She was in the same room as her father, and she was able to laugh about it. Granted, the fact that he was unaware of her presence made it easier. It was even a little bit fun, the sense of finally being the one holding all the cards. After all these years, she'd managed to get one over on him.

He came to a stop in the center of the room, where he was soon encircled by laughing, clapping attendees. Those not laughing held up their phones to take videos and pictures. Somebody handed him a microphone, and naturally, the first thing to come out of his mouth was, "Ho! Ho! Ho! Merry Christmas to all friends of the worthy charity we're here to support!" A thunderous round of applause followed this. Annie and Sam clapped if only to blend in. They didn't wear the same adoring expressions as those around them.

"On behalf of the organization and the many children whose lives will be forever changed thanks to your generosity, I say thank you. When I first became involved with them nearly twenty years ago, I couldn't have imagined the profound nature of the change these kids would have on my life..."

"My goodness." Annie rolled her eyes up at Sam. "Why wouldn't it be all about him, after all?"

"He's soaking it up, for sure." Though he didn't sound as exasperated as Annie felt. "It does help the kids, though."

"Of course. But he had another kid, one he fathered, who could've used his charity. Maybe even his presence." In fact, the more time she spent in the middle of this lavish party, the greater her irritation with the man at the center of it. Even if he'd supported her and her mother, it had barely been enough to keep them afloat. His generosity had only ever extended so far. Almost like he'd wanted to keep them needing him.

It wasn't until Gavin handed over the microphone and began making his way to his chair that Annie stirred from her reverie. "I think this is as good a time as any." She'd already started in his direction by the time Sam muttered a curse and hurried to catch up.

"You're not going to confront him like this, are you?" Annie heard him but didn't respond. There was no putting into words what she was feeling, anyway. If she didn't do it right that very minute, she might lose her nerve.

He had his back to them, arranging his sack of presents beside the chair. Most of the partygoers were taking their seats, prepared to dine, while a live band began to play softly. No one noticed Annie as she stepped up behind Santa—or if they did, they thought nothing of it.

She pulled in as deep a breath as she could and reminded herself she wasn't alone. Sam was behind her, ready to get them both out of there if things went south.

It's now or never.

"Excuse me, Santa? I've been waiting a long time to sit on your lap."

He froze, bent over the gifts. Satisfaction sparked in her chest, overshadowing the pounding of her heart. For once, she had surprised him.

Slowly he turned, eyes wide behind a pair of wire-rimmed spectacles. Eyes she'd never looked into before. Eyes filled with surprise—followed by understanding. "Hello, Annie."

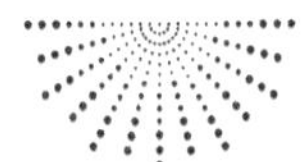

CHAPTER SIXTEEN

"I can walk on my own, thank you." Annie folded her arms when a tuxedoed man who would've looked more natural in a football uniform tried to take hold of her. This wasn't a museum security guard—rather, he and the man walking beside Sam were more likely Gavin's private guards.

Sure enough, he addressed them by name. "Jim, Frank, hands to yourselves." They were like trained dogs, obeying their master's orders.

Annie stared at the back of her father's head as they traveled a narrow hall between exhibit rooms. It was too surreal, seeing him dressed the way he was. Of all times for them to finally meet in person.

They came to a stop in a small room full of glass-cased artifacts. "Leave us alone." Gavin removed the costume spectacles and beard before placing them on a case. The hat and wig came next.

"You sure about that?" One of the two men jerked his chin toward Sam.

"He won't be a problem." Gavin looked at Sam while smoothing down his gray hair with both hands. "Will you?" His smile was too wide. Like a shark's.

"I'll behave if you do." Sam's smile was similar to Gavin's, as was the hard look in his eyes. There were no illusions here.

Once they were alone, Gavin shrugged affably. "You found me. Congratulations. You finally started putting your smarts to use after you dumped the dead weight you were carrying around."

So they were getting straight into it, then. No formalities, no introductions. And no pretending he wasn't entirely aware of her personal life. It was better this way. Less time wasted.

"Far be it from me to defend him, but you never met my ex-husband. How would you know?"

He held up a gloved finger. "Don't make assumptions. When did I say we never met?"

She should've known. "When?"

"Oh, years ago. I presented myself as an investor with a sure winner. The details don't matter." He sneered, shaking his head in what even a stranger could interpret as disgust. "He was too much of a coward to sign on. It was a surefire payday, but he got cold feet."

"You were going to give him money and pretend it was from investment dividends?" Edwin had never breathed a word of it to her. Yet another tidbit he hadn't seen fit to share.

"A man wants to care for his family. I had a daughter, a granddaughter. Why wouldn't I do everything in my power to provide what that loser couldn't?"

"We were always comfortable. We didn't need you."

"Just like you didn't need me so many other times? How about that college education my granddaughter is now receiving?"

"Nobody asked for your help."

"But you needed it, didn't you?" Gavin shot Sam a pointed look. "Most recently, you needed it two weeks ago. Was my concern such a curse then? I'd think you would thank me for butting in."

He was crafty, but then he would be. He'd made a career of crafting his image while being anything but who he pretended he was. "It's a good thing you were looking out then. I can admit it. But I want you to stop now. I'm a grown woman and I can handle myself."

"Can you? Since your move to North Carolina, how many brushes with death have you experienced? How many times have you been in danger?"

Frustration threatened to bring tears to her eyes. "You're not listening. All these years, you never saw fit to seek out a relationship with me, and now you can't be bothered to listen."

"Is that what this is about? You're angry with me for not playing the happy father?"

His choice of words—along with the snide tone in which he delivered them—strengthened her resolve. "I realize the idea is disgusting to you, but some men actually value being part of a family. And with everything Edwin did and all his lies, he's one thing you could never be: an engaged father."

"Spare me."

"You don't like hearing the truth? Then you'll hate this." She was shaking but took a step toward him just the same. "You could have done more for us, but you refused. You got my mother pregnant and made her marriage even more complicated than it already was. And you abandoned us both."

"I didn't abandon you. Who do you think provided for you?"

"Barely."

"Because she wouldn't accept more. I would have set you up anywhere she wanted, given you the best of everything—at least once I had it to give, but my fortune improved around the time you were in kindergarten. She refused more than the bare minimum."

"And why did she do that?"

A fraction of the light left his eyes. She knew the answer before he spoke. "She didn't approve of the way I made my money. Even if it meant giving you all the things you deserved, she wouldn't accept it."

It was the truth. She felt it in her bones. Why else would she feel as she did about Gavin's financial support? She'd been raised by a woman who hadn't wanted it any more than she did. "It's dirty money."

He scoffed. "Money is money. Do you think the power company cares where the money comes from when you pay your bill? The supermarket? The bank holding the note on your house?"

"I'm sure it makes you feel better, telling yourself this. It's how you rationalize what you do." Annie looked around, then waved a hand to indicate his costume. "And this. You tell yourself you're doing good for people."

"I am. Two things can be true at once. I build

careers. I put the right people in power. And I give back whenever I can."

"So why is your brother terrified of you?"

His lips twisted in a snarl. "That bum? You must be joking. You think I could allow him to get close to you? I would've threatened anything to keep him out of your life, and your mother's. The little bit of money she accepted to keep the two of you afloat wouldn't have stretched very far once he got his fingers on it."

There was no arguing with that.

Suddenly, his eyes widened, and his snarl softened into something closer to a smile. "You're wearing her pearls. I gave them to her."

She raised a hand to her throat. "You did?"

"I bought them for her when she told me—" His voice cracked, and he lowered his gaze to the floor. "When she told me she was going to have you. I would've given her a ring, but I couldn't very well do that when she already wore my brother's. I know how that sounds."

"She always treasured them."

They stared at each other for a moment. What was he thinking? Was he telling the truth? It occurred to her he could be making everything up. There was no one alive who could prove him wrong about the money he'd supposedly offered to the woman who'd borne his child.

Annie drew herself up to her full height and reminded herself what she was doing there. Why she'd gone to all this trouble. "She would want you to back off. Let me live my life. And for heaven's sake, stop taking revenge on the people who've hurt me."

"You're my daughter."

"By blood only. You have no room in my life unless you want me to make room. I don't appreciate you hovering over me like some avenging angel I never see or speak to."

"You mean I could beat the tar out of anybody who hurts you as long as I fly in to North Carolina to pay a visit every so often?"

"You know that isn't what I mean. I won't have your actions on my conscience, which is where they sit right now. And they always will. You can't talk me out of it."

He blew out a soft sigh. "You're so much like her. She couldn't help but give in to what grew between us, but she was too determined to live up to her vows. Too stuck in her principles to hitch her wagon to a man like me."

"I must be like her, since I completely understand

why she'd do what she did. You're not going to sweet talk me and you won't bribe me into it. Like that so-called anonymous donation of yours."

"Don't be a fool. You need that money to get back on your feet."

"I would rather have a father I could be proud of. Not one who hides behind spies and anonymous donations. And not one who hires men to beat strangers half to death or run them off the road."

"I protect what's mine." He didn't feign confusion or bother denying involvement.

"Then the next time something like that happens, I'll tell the police exactly who was behind it. I'm not playing around. You're going to stay out of my life unless you want to be there as a father. Not as a leg breaker or a bodyguard."

He pursed his lips, a flinty look touching his eyes. The look of a man accustomed to sizing up his opponent. "You want that?"

"To have a father? Yes. I would like that."

"Even a father like me?"

"I spent nearly all my life thinking Cal was my father. You think you're that much worse?"

His gaze drifted over her shoulder. "I have to get back to the party. People will start to wonder."

"I need you to tell me you're going to stop inter-fering. Please."

"Or else?" He raised an eyebrow. "What do you think you're going to do to stop me?"

"What do you think? I'll tell Melanie all about her grandfather. I'll ruin your image. Unless you want to run your own daughter off the road, you're not going to stop me."

"And me with her." Sam touched a hand to her back. "We aren't the only ones. If we never made it back home, others would know why."

"You must think I'm a real brute if you think I wouldn't let you make it home." Gavin began putting his costume back together, snickering as he did. "You're the only decent man she's ever been involved with. Though that fling with the kid? Not so smart."

Annie caught Sam scowling out of the corner of her eye. He kept his thoughts to himself, though there was practically steam billowing out of his ears.

"We'll go and leave you to your party." She took Sam's hand, squeezing it tight. It was easy to look and sound fierce with adrenaline pumping through her system, but adrenaline could only carry her so far—and the supply was starting to run low. "Please, think about what I said. And feel free to reach out any time. Give me a call if and when you decide to be a father. And a grandfather. I'm sure Mel would like to know you."

Gavin hesitated, pausing in the act of replacing his beard. "You mean that?"

"I might be a lot like Mom, but I'm not completely hardheaded." She backed away one slow step at a time, with Sam following suit. "We won't ruin your party or tell anybody why we're here. I only wanted to see you and get this off my chest."

One of Gavin's men stuck his head in the room. "They're asking for you in the ballroom."

"You'd better hurry up." It felt anticlimactic but there was nothing more she could do. "Goodbye. And happy holidays, I suppose."

"They'd be happier with my daughter and grand-daughter."

She almost stumbled out of surprise. He liked to throw last-second curveballs, didn't he? "I think it might be a little sudden this year. Next year could be a different story, though, but you'd have to start building a relationship soon."

He nodded slowly. "I'll take that under consid-eration."

"Come on." Sam gave her arm a slight tug. It was enough to get her moving. Now that it was over and she'd said her piece, she was nearly overcome by a strange sense of floating. Like a balloon that came free from a child's fist. She needed him to help her, guide her, to lead her out of the museum. Otherwise, she might've spent the night wandering from one room to another, helplessly lost.

"You did it. You were brave, and you did it." Sam helped her into her coat once they were outside, closing it tight before pulling her close. "I'm proud of you."

"He's only a man. Just an old man. I don't know what I was expecting." She leaned against him, grateful for his strength when she felt weak with relief.

"You did so well. You didn't even need me."

"That's not true." She tipped her head back, gazing up at him. "I couldn't have done it without you. Now, we'll see if he listens."

He took her arm and led her down the stairs. "Something tells me he will."

"Why do you say that?"

"If there was ever a lonelier man in existence, I wouldn't want to meet him. The way his eyes lit up at the idea of having a family?" He glanced over his shoulder, sighing. "He'll fall in line."

Strange, but Annie hoped he would. Gavin was her last connection to her mother, to her past. She hadn't understood until now how much that mattered.

"What do you say we go someplace for a nice dinner?" Sam pulled out his phone and opened an app. "The sky's the limit."

"How about we go back to the hotel and order too much food through room service?"

He grinned. "That sounds even better."

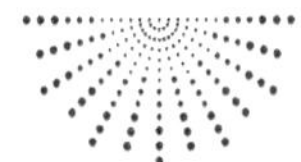

CHAPTER SEVENTEEN

"Cookies are done! Want me to put this other sheet in the oven?"

"Yes, please!" Annie plugged in the vacuum cleaner, the sight of which sent Bogart flying under the sofa. "It's your fur I have to vacuum up, you know. You could at least help."

"How long should they be in for?"

Good thing she hadn't turned the machine on before Tyler shouted his question. "Twelve minutes."

By the time Tyler entered the room, she was in the middle of vacuuming the armchair. "I thought you did that already this morning!"

She raised her voice the way he had. "I did, but I want to make sure it looks perfect."

He waited until she was finished to speak again.

"Everything already looks perfect. You've worked like a dog for days, cleaning the house from top to bottom. I'm pretty sure you have enough cookies in there to feed the entire block."

"I'm not trying to feed the block. Only half the block." She winked at the way he rolled his eyes. "Everybody was so nice, bringing food over after the fire. I want to show them how grateful I am. Besides, Mel loves my chocolate chip cookies."

"So I should lay off them until she gets here?"

"If I see one in your hand, I'll slap it right out." He winced before retreating to the kitchen once again. She called out after him. "Don't even think about stealing any now!"

There were fingerprints on the coffee table. Hadn't she wiped it down earlier? Why was it so difficult to keep things the way she wanted them? Once Melanie arrived and settled in, it wouldn't seem as important for the house to be pristine.

Why was she bending over backward to impress her daughter? A psychiatrist would have a field day.

"What time are you leaving for the airport?" Tyler came in carrying a stack of wrapped boxes which he placed beneath the tree.

"Your gifts look so much nicer than mine." Annie wrinkled her nose at the packages she'd wrapped, which looked somewhat like a toddler had done the job. "I've never been good at wrapping gifts neatly."

"It all gets ripped off, anyway."

He'd asked a question, hadn't he? Her mind was all over the place. "Her flight gets in at five, so I'll head out around four." That gave her another two hours to fret herself into a tizzy. Sam would come by for dinner later that evening—Annie had decided to order dinner from the same restaurant Mildred had used for Thanksgiving. They'd done a wonderful job and the arrangement would free her up to spend time with her daughter on Christmas Eve.

The last batch of cookies was fresh out of the oven when the doorbell rang. Tyler answered while Annie packaged up cooled cookies she'd baked earlier in the day.

"Merry Christmas!"

She didn't have to see the face to know the voice. "Mel?" Cookies forgotten, Annie rushed from the kitchen to find her beaming daughter standing in the living room.

"Surprise!" Melanie set her bags down before throwing her arms around her mother. "Gotcha!"

"What is this all about?" Annie didn't know whether to laugh or to cry with happiness. "How did you get here? I was supposed to pick you up at the airport later."

"I found another way to get here."

"What do you mean?"

"Um, Annie?" Tyler cleared his throat, pulling her attention toward him—and the man who'd stepped into the house.

Her stomach dropped. "Edwin."

"He insisted on driving me this morning instead of having me fly." Melanie grinned over her shoulder. "He said he wanted to spend as much time with me as possible."

While Annie didn't doubt his sincerity, she very much doubted this was the only reason he'd insisted on making the long drive. "Merry Christmas. Please, come in and make yourself at home." The words sounded like they were coming from somebody else's mouth. Certainly, they couldn't be coming from her. Not toward the man who'd hurt her so badly.

"I can't stay long." He even sounded the same, though why wouldn't he? It only made sense. Leave it to him to stun her like this.

"Can I get you anything to drink? I have roughly a million cookies in the kitchen."

"Ooh, including chocolate chip?" Melanie

bounced up and down on the balls of her feet, eyes shining.

"Come on. We'll grab some together." Tyler paused, though, extending a hand toward Edwin. "It's good to meet you."

"You, too." Edwin shoved his hands in his coat pockets after shaking Tyler's. Something on the floor fascinated him, evidently, since he couldn't stop staring at it.

Silence unfurled between them. Annie fervently wished somebody had warned her. There was flour on her already beat-up cleaning shirt, and she'd been halfway through munching on a butter cookie when the doorbell rang. There were probably crumbs around her mouth.

"This is my house. Would you like a tour?"

He shook his head but smiled as he raised it. "It's nice. Very nice. A good size, a nice neighborhood."

"Yes, the neighbors are nice." How many times could they use the word before it lost meaning? "We'd call them nosy up in Jersey, but I appreciate them keeping an eye out, too."

"And living with him is okay? You feel safe and all?"

"I wouldn't have asked our daughter to stay here over the holidays if I didn't feel safe."

"Of course." He offered a weak smile. "You can't blame a guy for worrying. Especially with so many disasters and near-tragedies going on around here."

"There it is." She spoke in a whisper for Melanie's sake, even though it sounded as though she and Tyler were having a ball in the kitchen and paid no attention to the living room. "I knew there had to be a reason for you to go to all this trouble. You wanted to look me in the face while criticizing me."

"Not at all."

"Please. It's what you thrived on throughout our marriage. Criticism. Not-so-subtle hints. Controlling everything in the house and pouting when you couldn't have your way."

He looked up at the ceiling, his cheeks puffing out in a familiar sigh. "I don't want to go through this. That's not why I'm here. I wanted to see for myself that you're safe and in one piece."

"You did?"

"Do you think it's easy, knowing I'm the reason you came down here in the first place? And ever since you arrived, it seems there's been one thing after another. You got shot. You nearly died more than once." He threw his hands into the air. "That never happened back when we were married."

"You think the things that happened to me are your fault?"

"It's my fault we fell apart."

The room started spinning. Her brain couldn't seem to process what she was hearing. The idea of this coming from Edwin was as believable as Santa Claus himself. Yet he seemed serious. Contrite. "You mean that?"

Another sigh, this one softer. His cheeks colored while frown lines bracketed his mouth. "You find out your ex-wife nearly died—more than once—and things have a way of looking different. You start seeing the past through clear eyes. No matter how I blamed you for the spying, there would've been nothing to spy about if I hadn't sneaked around."

Her mouth worked, but no sound came out. She stood there sputtering for a moment before he took pity. "I know it's a surprise. I wanted to be sure I told you in person that I know it was all my fault, and I'm sorry."

"I don't know what to say. Thank you, I guess? I appreciate your candor."

"I appreciate you not throwing me out on my ear." They shared a quiet laugh. "I know this was a surprise. I doubted you'd agree to my driving down if you knew in advance."

"I have a little experience with showing up unexpected, myself." She motioned for him to sit down, and she joined him on the sofa. There was a healthy amount of space between them, and it was still by far the closest they'd been in a long time.

"I want you to know something." She looked him straight in the eye for the first time in ages. It wasn't easy to put aside the many, many times she'd gazed into those eyes with love. How many hours had they spent sitting together in front of the Christmas tree over the course of their marriage? Now they were in her home, one he had nothing to do with. How surreal it all was, especially when there'd been no time to prepare herself mentally. "I'm very happy with the way my life is now."

His brows lifted. "Sincerely?"

"Sincerely. I'm proud of the store. Proud of my home. I've made friends. It isn't a flashy life, but it's mine."

Maybe it was the tree and the lights. The presents. The sound of Melanie giggling in the kitchen, filling the house with warmth. The idea of having nearly two full weeks with her daughter for the first time in far too long.

Whatever the reason, Annie's heart swelled.

There was nothing wrong with being generous, nothing weak about extending an olive branch.

"I forgive you. I want you to know that."

He exhaled hard, like a man who had been punched in the stomach.

"Not that I think you came here asking for forgiveness, and I can't assume you want it. But I thought just in case, if you ever wished you had it down the line. It's yours. You didn't force me into this life. You helped me into it." She stopped short of saying she was glad he had, since there was no glossing over the pain of his betrayal and everything that came after. It had caused Melanie so much pain, as well, and neither of them could ignore that.

But she now understood that while she lived a simple life in a small town, her world had become so much bigger than she could have imagined only a few years ago. There were so many new people comprising her world, all of them willing to go out of their way to support her. She had rediscovered herself and proven how brave she could be.

She had found a new family.

It was Edwin's turn to sputter, and he did, and for so long Annie took pity on him. "You don't have to say anything. Or if you think of something on the road, don't hesitate to give me a call." He nearly beamed with gratitude as they stood, with Annie calling Melanie into the room to say goodbye to her father. He had a long drive ahead of him, and his own family to get home to.

She and Melanie watched from the front door as he walked to the car.

"Everything okay?" There was so much hope in Melanie's voice, it almost broke her mother's heart.

"Everything is fine. I don't envy him the amount of driving he has in front of him, and on Christmas Eve. He'll be lucky if he gets home before midnight."

"I don't know. It was, like, super important to him. He made his mind up."

Annie sighed while lifting an arm to wave goodbye. "That sounds like him." They waited until Edwin was out of the driveway before closing the door. She pulled Melanie in for another hug. "Come on. Let me show you around. Maybe we can drop some of these cookies off before Sam comes over, and you can meet some of the neighbors."

Tyler pulled her aside. "Are you alright?"

"Better than alright." It was too much to put into words all at once, especially with Melanie there. Was it closure? She had never expected it or even hoped for it, telling herself some things were better off left alone. Now, she understood how much she'd longed to have one final word with Edwin about the disaster their marriage had become.

It was obvious their conversation had taken this long to come around because she had needed to first establish herself, to put herself in a place where she could forgive him for what he had done. She'd needed to grow, and now she had, and there was room in her life for forgiveness.

"I think I'll come around with you." Tyler loaded a few boxes of cookies into a canvas bag, then went to the living room for his coat. "If anything, having me along will discourage those chatterbox neighbors from talking your ear off. You'll be out there until tomorrow morning otherwise."

"And it wouldn't hurt your business if they see you and remember they need help with projects around the house, either." Melanie grinned at Annie behind Tyler's back.

He grumbled, but there was a twinkle in his eye when he opened the door for them. "College kids. Thinking they know everything."

Even with Tyler coming along, the sun was setting by the time the three of them returned to the house. "You now know more than you ever wanted to about my neighbors." Annie chuckled in sympathy, draping an arm around her daughter's waist.

"It was nice. I didn't know there were so many friendly people."

"Nosy people, you mean." Tyler shrugged when Annie rolled her eyes at him. "What? They've been dying to get a look at the kid ever since they found out you have one."

Annie was about to remind him that three of the neighbors they'd visited mentioned needing his handyman services, but the sight of Sam's approaching car stole the thought. "He's early."

"Sam? Is that his car?" Melanie laughed at the sight of Annie's face. "You look like you saw a ghost. It's going to be even more fun than I thought, meeting him."

Here she was. Standing in her driveway, waiting to introduce her daughter to her boyfriend. Was he her boyfriend? Considering they'd spent the past few weekends together and she now had a dedicated drawer in the nightstand, she supposed he was.

Only it wasn't Sam's appearance that made her heart leap with joy.

It was Mildred. Sam helped her climb out of the seat of his low-slung sports car, and Tyler jogged over to take her other arm. "Escorted by two young men. I feel like a movie star."

"Mildred." Annie's eyes filled with tears as the

three of them approached. "I didn't think you'd make it."

"And miss the opportunity to meet this young woman?" Mildred beamed at Melanie. "How could I do that? Not when I figured there would never be a reason to enjoy the holidays again. I decided I need to take advantage of the good times while I can."

Sam exchanged a look with Annie. "If those aren't words to live by, I don't know what is."

Neither did she.

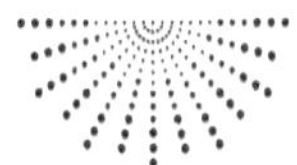

"Wow." Melanie leaned against the front counter, propping her chin on her hands as she looked around the store. "It looks even better now than it did in the pictures you sent. I mean, no offense or whatever, but the fire might've been a blessing in disguise."

Annie frowned at her daughter's choice of words. "Thank you very much."

"You know what I mean. It was a reason to freshen the place up. And you had all that money from the fundraiser to cover it."

"So what if I nearly died?"

"Pretend I never said anything."

The fact was, Melanie had a point. The fire had been an excuse to paint the walls, refinish the floors, everything Annie had wished to do but imagined wouldn't be possible for years. She'd invested in new bookshelves, new lights, and now the store looked fresh and clean. Even modern.

Throughout the week, Melanie had teased the store's reopening across social media. While Annie had at first shied away from the photos of them stocking the shelves, Melanie had eventually gotten through to her. "Customers want to know about the people behind the business. The better they know you, the more they'll like you and want to give you their business."

Sometimes she wondered if her daughter would be better at running the store than she was. Maybe someday the store would be hers, come to think of it. It only made sense, keeping it in the family.

That wouldn't be for a long time. Now that she had a virtually brand-new store, a boyfriend who got along tremendously with her daughter, and so many other things going for her, she'd go out of her way to avoid dangerous people and situations.

"Now, if you would only tell me where the money came from."

Annie's head swung around. "What?"

"Come on." Melanie scoffed, rolling her eyes. "I've heard you and Tyler muttering back and forth when you think I'm not paying attention. I've noticed the looks you give each other, too. You're hiding something, and Tyler keeps trying to convince you to fess up. It always comes up when you're talking about what else you can afford for the store."

There was no point in lying. That much was clear. Melanie had always been sharp, observant. "It's not as if I didn't want to tell you. I planned to do it before you left. I promise."

"What, on the way to the airport?"

"Melanie." She shook her head, disapproving. "It can be just as difficult for an adult to talk about things as it is for a person your age."

"I'm an adult, too."

"Says you."

Melanie growled, but was grinning. "Come on. Start the new year fresh. No secrets. It can't be all that bad."

"I found my father. I went out to see him. He's who the money came from—though he donated before I visited him." Why it seemed so important to make that clear, she didn't know.

Melanie plopped down on the stool behind the register. "Oh."

"Not prepared for that, were you?"

"How could I have been? So he's got a lot of money? Is he really rich? Why didn't you ever meet him before? Can I meet him?" And finally, the question behind Annie's hesitation. "Why didn't you tell me before now?"

"It's complicated." When it was clear that wouldn't be enough, Annie did her best to explain. She told her of the times Gavin had stepped into her life uninvited. How her mother hadn't wanted a relationship with him once he got involved with sketchy, unscrupulous people. How she had been just as worried about meeting him and getting mixed up in his world.

"He does want a relationship with both of us—if we want it too." Annie watched her daughter closely, waiting for any sign she was upset or confused. "I told him he has to quit sticking his nose in from thousands of miles away, like he's been doing all this time. No more watching, no more punishing people."

"I mean…" Melanie blew out a heavy sigh, slumping a little. "It's not like I didn't wish I could kill whoever set the store on fire. I did. A lot."

"He's used to getting his way, no matter what it takes or costs. That's something we both have to keep in mind. Can we overlook the things he's done?"

"I mean, he did it because he loves you."

The innocence of youth. She wanted so badly to believe her grandfather was a loving man. Maybe he could be. He hadn't been given much of a chance. But Annie had heard the relief in his voice when she'd talked about being a family.

"It's up to you whether you want to know him better. I'm sure he wants to know you." She put an arm around her daughter's shoulders and squeezed, but was careful to step back and give her room. "No pressure."

"Thanks." She looked troubled, teeth sunk into her lip as she mulled it over. This wasn't a decision Annie could make for her, no matter how she wished she could. It wasn't easy, but then neither was growing up.

"Looks like that was the last of the boxes." Sam emerged from the basement, brushing dust from his shoulders. Tyler followed close behind. It seemed like Melanie's presence gave them a reason to get along better—Annie hoped that would remain the case once she went back to school.

"We'd better hurry up and head home to get ready for Mildred's." Tyler shook out his hair. "I'm pretty sure a dozen spiders decided to adopt me as their new home. Can't be bringing them to her house as a New Year's surprise."

"I hope she doesn't mind having us all there." Melanie put on her coat while Annie turned out the lights.

"She loves it. And it's easier for her than leaving the house." Sam held out Annie's coat, helping her into it. "She did well last week, but I think it will take time before she's comfortable going out regularly."

The weight of his hands on her shoulders was a comfort. She placed her hands over them and looked up at him with a smile. "Thank you for all your help. Nobody wants to spend their time off lugging boxes up from a musty cellar."

"You know it's worthwhile if it means helping you." He shot a look toward Tyler and Melanie, who were discussing social media plans and paying no attention, then lowered his head to murmur close to her ear. "Though I plan to collect my fee once you're free to spend the night again."

As much as she wished Melanie never had to leave, at least there were consolations.

"Hurry up! It's one minute to midnight!" Melanie waved Annie and Mildred in from the kitchen. The TV was tuned to the festivities in Times Square. Tyler poured champagne while Sam passed around paper hats and noisemakers.

Mildred's cheeks were pink with excitement. "I haven't so looked forward to a new year in as long as I can remember."

"Not even when Aunt Hattie was alive?" Melanie and Mildred had done a lot of talking about Annie's aunt over the past week.

"It wasn't the same as this. You reach a certain age and you don't have so many things to look forward to anymore. No goals to reach for beyond staying alive another year." She patted Melanie's cheek, smiling fondly. "Now I have you to keep in touch with, and your mother, and your cousin. I get to watch all of you grow and thrive, and it's a privilege."

Annie's eyes filled with tears which she barely blinked back. She couldn't have explained to Mildred how much she meant if given all night to do it. Close friend, second mother, confidant. She settled on a tight hug for the time being.

"Thirty seconds." Sam joined her with a glass of

champagne in both hands. "Any resolutions for the new year?"

"Let's start with no near-death experiences."

"Oh, please, don't break that one." They shared a quiet laugh, gently touching their glasses in a toast. Neither of them needed to go into detail when it came to what they were thinking. The coming year, and all the years after, held nothing but promise for them—both individually and as a couple.

The store would re-open in two days, and there was no reason to believe it would be anything less than a success after all the work Melanie had put into advertising it.

Tyler's business was on the verge of a boom. He was beginning to find his place in the community, ready to move on from the past.

Her relationship with Melanie had never been better, and there was hope for a relationship with Gavin on the horizon as well.

She would never have believed it if someone had told her a year ago that life would be so dramatically different, that she would usher in the new year surrounded by laughter and love—and hope. Now, with Sam's arm around her and Melanie at her other side, it was time to do just that.

"Three... two... one... Happy new year!" They

blew their horns, cheering the way the people on TV did. After kissing Melanie's cheek, Annie turned toward Sam and tipped her head back for a kiss.

"You ready for this?" He smiled down at her, his eyes warm.

Though she doubted he was talking about a simple new year's kiss, she didn't need to think about her response. "Absolutely."

For more Winnie Reed books click here!

Sign up for the newsletter to be notified of new releases.

Click on link for
Newsletter